LIGHT OF T.
BOOK THREE OF THE
SERI.

Robert Ryan

Cover Design by www.damonza.com

ISBN-13 978-0-9942054-9-0
(print edition)

Trotting Fox Press

Contents

1. Stillness in the Storm

Gil drew his sword, and the hiss of steel as it slid from the leather scabbard was the whisper of death in his ear. Now that he had drawn the blade, he must use it. That was the first rule of fighting. Avoid drawing to the last, but having drawn be prepared to kill. Or be killed.

He was now caught in a fight to the death. It was not of his choosing. It was neither his plan nor his purpose. But none of that mattered. His opponent had set this in motion, and having begun it must end in blood.

The day was bright and sunny. The sky suddenly blue beyond compare. The touch of air against his skin was a caress, and everything seemed alive and vibrant. He knew this was because he might die, and his mind was suddenly aware of all the things he could lose. But beyond that loomed the threat of the great dark, of the unknown, of death and oblivion. It stabbed fear through him. He felt that too, felt the tightening of his muscles and the churning of his stomach, felt it all with unsurpassed clarity.

He did not like it. But all that he felt, his opponent felt also, and that helped to steady him. He was not going to die here today, not if he could help it.

His opponent made a move. It was a feint, a mere ripple of motion intended to make Gil react. And he did, stepping smoothly to the side.

The dance had begun. This early period in a fight was a chance to observe how the enemy moved, which foot they favored, how they advanced and retreated. It was an opportunity to appraise the enemy and discover a weakness, and one always existed.

There would be no rushed battle here. This was a duel, and one between accomplished swordsmen. No chances would be taken and no gambles on surprise or trickery considered. Not until they each had the measure of the other, not until one had the upper hand and the other was forced to try luck rather than rely on skill.

His opponent glided forward on practiced footwork, the tip of his sword thrusting. Gil rocked back, allowing his rear foot to hold his weight while his own sword deflected the strike. In the same motion, he sent a slashing riposte toward his adversary's throat.

The man parried it with ease, and the sound of steel on steel rang loudly. Gil did not mind. This too was part of the testing. He had learned that his opponent favored blocking rather than deflection.

They circled each other now. Eyes focused, concentration intense. Each step assessed, every movement of waist and limb studied for telltale signs of an impending strike.

Gil noticed the man watched his eyes. This was a tactic used for intimidation. And well might his opponent do so, for he was older, stronger and more experienced. Gil, in his turn, ignored it and kept his gaze at the center of the man's chest. From here, he could best see his enemy's feet and shoulder, which were often the first part of the body to move before a thrust or slash.

His enemy nimbly altered his footwork and began to circle in the opposite direction. Gil flowed smoothly with the change, knowing that if he had not done so the man would have attacked seeking to strike while he was off balance.

The cottage came into view behind his enemy, and the ploughed field beyond it. The building, though tidy and bordered by a colorful flower bed, was small and only had thatch roofing. It was not the kind of place that a member of the nobility would have much time for, and it must have discomfited Dernbrael that he had been forced into hiding here after his treacherous plot to usurp the throne failed. Gil had felt the man's shame on his discovery, but was there a way to use that emotion against him now that this duel had begun?

Dernbrael dropped low and slashed his blade at Gil's knees. Gil shuffled back, avoiding the dangerous strike, and not falling for the trap. Had he dodged and then leapt in to land a powerful overhand strike while his enemy was in a seemingly vulnerable position, he would have driven himself onto the follow-up strike – a disemboweling flick of the wrist.

Dernbrael stepped back and grinned. "Brand taught you well. He'll not be to blame for your death. But think on this, boy. You *will* die. And you have no heir. Your line will end with you, and Cardoroth will have a new king." He pointed with his sword. "It will all be for the best. You are *elùgrune,* boy. Nightborn. A thing of evil and no good can come from your life."

Gil felt a rush of blood to his face, and the pale marks on his palms itched, but he did not answer. He was not experienced, but he knew when he was being goaded. He would *not* react rashly, even if he felt the barb. He forced a grin instead, and held his blade steady before him.

Dernbrael attacked anyway, launching a vicious overhand strike intended to split Gil's skull. This time Gil blocked, for there was no safe way to deflect such a blow as that. Steel cracked against steel. The jolt of impact rocked him, and he was forced into a clumsy step backward. Straightaway Dernbrael followed through, trying a slashing technique for the throat.

Gil neither blocked nor deflected it. He sidestepped and began to circle again. He was patient, perhaps more patient than his opponent, and there was no rush.

Dernbrael would have expected a counter attack, for a man attacked usually retaliated in kind. But Brand had taught him better than that.

The cottage and field were now behind Gil. Ahead of him, to the rear of his enemy, stood the ten Durlin guards and the fifty soldiers that had come with him out of the city to arrest Dernbrael. This fight was unnecessary, and he could end it now by a mere signal to his men. That was tempting, for the fear of death was upon him, but he had agreed to Dernbrael's demand to duel for a reason.

The rogue noble launched another attack. This was no mere testing strike, no probe of defenses: it was a sustained drive of blow after blow, each potentially deadly and all executed with skill and burning ferocity.

Gil swayed and stepped. He used movement as his first protection, evading rather than deflecting or parrying. But it was not enough. The enemy had his measure now, had learned his method of fighting and drove his blistering offense with precision. Gil was forced to not just deflect but also to block. This was not to his advantage because the other man was stronger, but almost as though Dernbrael could read his mind each jab and slash arrived just that little bit too fast for him, and always at the angle that was hardest to deal with.

Panic rose in Gil. His body grew tense and that ate away at the nimbleness of his footwork. His sword arm stiffened too, and this made his defense slower and more vulnerable.

But the other man was older, and his breathing began to quicken now. He slashed once more, a backhanded riposte that nearly tore away Gil's throat, and then stepped back.

They did not speak. The two of them gazed at each other. There was hatred in Dernbrael's eyes, but there was confidence too. It annoyed Gil, for the man thought he was the better swordsman. He believed it was just a matter of time and then, and then who knew? Did he think that having killed the heir to the throne he could survive being arrested? Did he believe he was still a chance of winning a trial, proving his innocence and then even being crowned king by the nobles? It was foolish, and yet with Gil dead and the threat of war on the horizon … anything was possible.

Gil nearly withdrew. Why had he agreed to this duel? But that was fear clouding his thoughts. He knew exactly why he had accepted the challenge.

When he had come with his men and called Dernbrael out of the cottage, hatred had flared on both sides. This was something personal between them, something more than justice and ambition. That alone was enough to stir up a fight, but there was more.

War loomed, sooner or later. Brand remained regent, but the time would come when he was not there. Then the people would look to their king, a young king, inexperienced and newly crowned. He would be vulnerable then. The plotting of the nobles would not cease. The morale of the people would erode. It was better to send a message now, to establish his reputation. And Dernbrael had given him that opportunity by challenging him to a duel. In this, Gil could show himself as an energetic leader of strength and courage. One able to personally fight his enemies. He was no callow youth, but a leader worthy of a long line of warriors.

Dernbrael had caught his breath. "So, boy. How did you find me here?"

Gil ignored being called a boy. It was another attempt to goad him. Nor was he going to be caught off guard. He stepped back, ensuring the other man could not launch into an attack while they spoke. Even as he did so, he read a flicker of annoyance on the other man's face at this precaution.

It was a pleasing reaction, for it showed that Dernbrael could himself be thrown off balance mentally. Gil noted it, and allowed himself a faint grin while he replied to the question.

"It does not matter," he said. "You are found, and you will be dealt with."

He knew that not giving a proper answer would annoy Dernbrael. It would only be natural for him to speculate if he had been betrayed by someone he trusted, and that would upset him. Goading worked both ways.

Dernbrael shrugged with seeming nonchalance, and then hurled himself into another attack. Gil had provoked it, even guessed that it would come, and he remained calm. This time he was better able to maneuver, using skill and footwork to avoid the deadly assault and deflecting the blade when he could not. Sometimes he was forced to block, but that was to be expected. They fought with long swords, and they were not weapons of great finesse.

All the while he obtained a better feel for his opponent. How the man moved. How he thought. But not as much as he wished. Dernbrael was experienced. He followed no set pattern. He attacked wherever he sensed there may be a weakness, and he probed it with relentlessness. Gil realized that even that was a pattern though. The rogue noble liked to attack. He liked to dominate. He was a man of confidence and authority. The question was, how could this be turned against him?

Gil became even more defensive. He relaxed, sinking deep into his own mind. There was only the movement of swords and the rhythm of his footwork. Neither fear nor hope existed. His mind did not get in the way of his training, and the skills his body had learned blossomed.

Muscles and reflexes were faster and surer than the conscious mind. That was what Brand had taught him. *Stillness in the storm*, the regent had called it. That state where the mind floated above the turmoil of the body and allowed it to move efficiently, unhindered by distress or desire.

Gil's patience provoked the intended result. Dernbrael, frustrated at not being able to exert control over the situation and engender fear, attacked once more. But this time he did so with wild hatred burning in his eyes.

The man moved swiftly. He slashed at Gil's throat and the blade hissed through the air only inches from delivering a death wound. Gil swayed back, and Dernbrael followed up with a brutal backhanded jab at his head.

Gil retreated. Dernbrael followed, pressing home his attack with a series of lightning-fast techniques. If he had been fast before, he was faster now. Anger drove him, and caution was lessened.

The rogue noble slashed again, but having missed he kicked out, nearly striking Gil in the groin. Gil stepped back and then to the side, narrowly avoiding another overhand strike.

With an agile pivot of his feet, Dernbrael thrust the tip of his blade at Gil's stomach. It was too fast, too unexpected for Gil to avoid, but he smashed down his own sword just in time. The two blades screeched as metal hammered into metal and sparks flew.

Dernbrael flicked his wrists and his blade slashed unopposed towards Gil's throat. But Gil was already moving, anticipating the technique and stepping to the side just in time. He was barely aware of anything except this life-and-death struggle, but he sensed the unease of the Durlin watching.

Dernbrael did not follow him this time. He stepped back, seeking another rest. Only his eyes still held their fury and gave Gil warning. Even as the man moved back he swiftly drew a dagger from a hidden arm-sheath and flung it.

Gil dodged to the side, but the dagger struck him with a sickening thump. Pain shot through him, and his left shoulder felt as though it were on fire, but it had only been a glancing blow and the dagger dropped to the ground.

It was not enough to break Gil's concentration. He remained alert, his sword held high before him and poised to defend or strike. His readiness forestalled the follow-up attack that Dernbrael had planned on, and hatred and frustration twisted his face.

Gil glanced at the dagger on the ground, and then he looked Dernbrael in the eyes.

"Ah yes, of course. A Duthenor dagger. I'm not sure throwing it in a duel fits well with the chivalry of the nobles. But no matter. More to the point, where are your allies now?"

Dernbrael ignored the questioning of his honor. "They know how to take care of themselves. They'll appear when Brand least expects it ... and he will surely die. The Duthenor have an ally beside me."

Gil nodded slowly, breathing deep of the fresh air that smelled of the ploughed field behind the cottage. He would use this moment of rest to purpose.

"The ally you speak of would be one of the Horsemen?" he said casually.

It was with satisfaction that he saw understanding in Dernbrael's eyes. He knew of the Horseman and his presence in the city, had probably even arranged for his covert entry. This took his treason to a higher level.

Gil went on. "But you should know this. Since you have been hiding like a rat down a hole, things have changed in the city. The Duthenor assassins were discovered. Brand dealt with them. And the Horseman, in case you were wondering, is dead also."

For the first time, Dernbrael showed uncertainty. This was news to him, and in a single moment he sensed all his plans and his last hope crashing down around him.

It was Gil's opportunity, and he grasped it. Shifting from defense to offense, he leapt forward, his blade gleaming in his hand. Swords flashed and the clang of steel on steel shattered the air. Dernbrael fell back, unprepared and surprised, yet still a master swordsman.

The sound of riders swiftly approaching broke through Gil's concentration. He had no idea if they were friends or enemies, but he had no chance to look.

Dernbrael unleashed a powerful beheading stroke. Gil anticipated it by the surge of anger that flared in the other man's eyes. Angry men struck for the head. He slipped under the wicked blow and drove his own blade upward. The point slid through cloth and flesh, and then Gil angled it upward to reach the heart and lungs.

Dernbrael stiffened and cried out. Then, knowing himself dead, and driven by hatred, he forced himself forward. He was too close to use his blade, but he smashed the pommel into Gil's head.

Gil felt a roar of pain. The world went dark and spun in circles. His knees wobbled, and he nearly fainted, but the blow had not quite struck him cleanly and he did not pass out. Instead, he gathered himself and then surged forward, kicking Dernbrael from him and keeping a tight grip on his sword. But even as he moved he felt that the weight of Dernbrael was a dead weight.

The nobleman sprawled to the ground. Blood and froth foamed at his mouth, but he no longer drew breath.

Gil swayed where he stood, his sword slick with the dead man's blood. "So is justice done," he said. "And as you fell, so too shall all who betray Cardoroth."

One of the Durlin came to him. He drew a white cloth from an inner pocket of his surcoat and handed it over. Gil dabbed it at the side of his head, feeling the pain there begin to throb. Looking at the cloth, he saw it was stained by blood.

"Keep holding it firmly in place," the Durlin advised. "It'll stop the bleeding."

Gil did so. He had not realized how badly he had been hit and how much blood there was. But the pain kept growing the more that he thought about it.

He turned to the riders who had come. There were two of them. He saw first that they possessed quality mounts. They were sleek animals, well cared for, fit and of the finest breeding. When he looked higher, taking in those who rode them, he understood why. These were messengers. They wore the gray cloaks customary to the army, but they were pinned with brooches that signaled their role as messengers: a hawk with wings half folded as though stooping through the sky toward prey. It signified speed, the kind that the mounts of the messengers by necessity must possess.

The two riders dismounted and approached Gil. Two Durlin separated from their companions and walked beside them.

"What is the watchword, gentlemen," Gil asked.

"Conhain," answered the man on the left. Then both men saluted. Gil returned it. The protocol had been fulfilled, and these men were as they appeared and not misinformants.

"Your Royal Highness," the man on the left spoke again. "The regent has sent us."

"What news?" Gil asked.

"This, sir. The scouts you sent out have returned. They bring word of an army. It is still many leagues to the north, but the regent believes its destination is Cardoroth. The army is large. Some thirty thousand, though it may yet increase. The regent bids you to return to the city as swiftly as your … your business here is taken care of."

The man's eyes strayed to Dernbrael's corpse. No doubt he would have known him as the rebel noble had been a general in the army.

Gil nodded. He pointed to a wooden trough by the side of the cabin. "Best water your horses. Then return to Brand. Tell him the traitor Dernbrael is dead, and that I will return close behind you."

The two messengers saluted, gathered the reins of their horses and led them to the trough.

Gil looked down once more on Dernbrael's corpse. How could Cardoroth survive? There were enemies from within who plotted for their own benefit. There were traitors who conspired with outside forces. And there was now a vast army set to march upon the city and destroy it.

He took the cloth from his head. It was covered in congealed blood. The risk he had taken was extreme, and yet the soldiers would spread the story. That was something at least, some gain from today's events. His reputation was begun, and it must now continue to grow. More than ever the people needed to believe in him. Brand remained regent, and there was none better to lead them into war. But Brand could be killed. It was time that

13

Gil stood up and showed himself as the king-to-be. If the morale of the people faltered, the enemy would overrun them. He gazed at Dernbrael's lifeless body. Blood had spilled from his wound onto the dirt, and flies crawled over his skin. If Cardoroth did not hold strong, such a fate awaited the entire city.

2. Born of the Dark

Gil hastened back to Cardoroth. The messengers were some half an hour ahead of him, but the news they had brought was on his mind. The much-feared war had at last eventuated. All he knew, all he loved, was in jeopardy.

His head still ached. It had taken some while to still the bleeding, and also to bandage his shoulder wound. It had taken just as long to find a blanket in which to wrap the body of Dernbrael, and then strap it over a horse. The rebel noble would come home too, but not as the king he had dreamed of to the last. He would return as a traitor, his body handed over to his family for burial. In this way he could serve Gil. It would help fuel word of what happened to traitors and spread the story of Gil's fight.

It was all something to think about. It could have been Gil himself there, tied to a horse and seeping blood into a blanket.

He breathed in of the country air as his horse trotted ahead. Ploughed fields lined each side of the road, and there were cottages much like the one in which Dernbrael had hidden. There were people too, unaware of what had happened or who these passing riders were. But many of them waved. Country friendliness at its best, and something that would not happen in the city. For all that it was a rougher life here, perhaps it was better. The sun shone, the wind blew and rain fell. Survival could be a struggle, as it was anywhere, but these people were untroubled by schemes and treachery and assassins.

Gil sighed. They did not have reputations to build and wars to win either. That was his job, and one that he did not like. But it was his duty, and he would no more shirk it than a farmer would shirk hitching his horses to the plough and working a hard day under a hot sun.

"You're still bleeding," the Durlin to his side said.

"It could be worse," Gil replied. He did not ask where he was bleeding from. He had felt blood wet both the bandage to his head and the one to his shoulder ever since he had started to ride. The constant motion was not good for wounds. But ahead, the South Gate to the city was just visible, and soon he could wash and change the blood-soaked bandages.

The road widened and they drew near. The South Gate was clearly visible now. The old name for it was Unlach Neben. And it truly was an old gate, as each of the four main gates were. It was said they were the original gates, constructed when the city wall was built. Gil believed it. He knew also that no enemy in the long history of the realm had ever forced their way though. He hoped it remained that way.

The gold representation of the sun upon it gleamed brightly. It was said to signify the sun beating down upon a faraway desert land. This was supposed to be the homeland of the elugs, whence the gold of the sun was obtained by an adventurer of old. Whether that was true or not, Gil had never learned.

Even as the glint of gold drew his gaze, something else distracted him. The air shimmered on the road before the gate. It seemed like a heat mirage, and yet Gil felt the sudden prickle of his skin and knew it was not. It was sorcery, and he raised his hand, fist clenched.

"Halt!" he commanded, and the column of riders drew to a swift stop.

Out of the shimmery air stepped a tall figure. Thin she was, black-haired and beautiful. As always, she had the bearing of a queen. All she needed was a crown and scepter.

Instead, she carried a wych-wood staff. It was Ginsar, and Gil felt the prickles on his skin turn to needles of ice.

The Durlin nudged their horses to gather close around him, and drew their swords. They had seen her before and knew who she was.

Ginsar tilted her head as though curious. "Why so scared?"

"We know you, witch," one of the Durlin answered. "Stay back!"

She studied him a moment. "And if I choose not to?" she answered, taking a slow step forward.

"Don't be alarmed," Gil said. "She can do no harm. This is an image only, and the true Ginsar is hiding in some dark grotto in the forest about the lake."

Ginsar turned her gaze to him, and her expressive eyes sparkled.

"My, haven't *you* grown. And however did you know? The casting of an image, and therefore the discernment of one, is beyond your skill. You surprise me."

"I know, Ginsar. That is enough."

She gazed at him speculatively a moment longer. "It's of no matter."

Gil sat straight in the saddle. "Speak," he said, "and then begone. I don't have all day to prattle with crazy ladies."

The witch's eyes flashed. "Crazy, is it? Well, perhaps I am." Her face softened and she laughed. "But I know a thing or two. Was not the great Shurilgar my master? Have

17

I not lived since the birth of Cardoroth itself? I am old, though in truth I do not appear so."

She held the backs of her hands up to her face, studied them a moment, and then winked at him.

"I am old, and steeped in wisdom that you would not fathom in a hundred years from now. And I know secrets. Oh yes, plenty of them. It would pay you to show respect."

Gil shrugged. He did not know what she intended here, but she had not come without purpose. Only by talking to her could he discover it. And perhaps, by talking, she would reveal more to him of her plans than she intended.

"Then speak, Ginsar. And say what you will. Then I will ride on and you will return to your shadow-haunted forest."

"So sure of yourself? You have another option, you know."

"And what's that?"

"Come to the shadow-haunted forest yourself. It's beautiful there, and there are secrets within it that would make your heart sing. Truly, I'm not lying to you."

Gil frowned, surprised by her words. "I think you really are crazy. Why would I go there?"

"Because it is where you belong. What better reason could there be?"

Gil shook his head. "No. I don't belong there at all."

"Again, always so sure of yourself. But you don't know what I know, nor do you see what I see. You are far more *shadow-haunted*, as you put it, than you admit to yourself. Did you not find it easy enough to kill Dernbrael?"

The words hung in the air, and Gil had no answer. How did she know Dernbrael was dead, let alone how? Her scry basin, perhaps. Or maybe she was linked to Dernbrael by sorcery. She may have met him. That made sense. Likely, she even encouraged his ambition for the

18

throne and fomented his treason. Such a link might have enabled her to watch over him with some degree of regularity. Otherwise the scry-magic was unpredictable. It rarely showed what the user wanted, and then only glimpses.

Gil had no answers to any of the questions his whirling mind posed, but he knew he had to reply.

"He was a traitor. He challenged *me*, and he died. It's that simple."

"Simple, is it now? Well, if you want simplicity, try this. The man died, but he need not have. His challenge was of no consequence. You could have overcome him. You had the men. No, Prince Gilcarist. You are elùgrune. Born of the dark. You *wanted* to kill him. Come to me, where you belong."

Gil understood her purpose now. At least, it seemed likely enough what it was. There were many people listening to what she said, and her words would spread through the city. It would cause distrust of him, and that would serve her during the war.

"I'm not elùgrune. I would die for my people. And this conversation is ended."

He reached out with his mind and felt the warmth in the air. There had been no heat mirage before, but now he made one. So strong was his reaction to her words that the air about the image of Ginsar crackled like a leaf thrown on flame and disappeared. Light flashed and thunder rumbled as though welling from the earth.

Gil hated using lòhrengai in public. Few knew he possessed the use of magic, but that number had increased rapidly lately. Now, the whole city would know. Perhaps that had been part of Ginsar's plan as well, but there was nothing he could do about it.

He signaled the column forward again, and nudged his horse into a trot. He did not need to look around to know

19

the eyes of the men were upon him. Ginsar had seen to that. If it were not enough that she had called him elùgrune, he had proved it to them himself.

The Durlin had already known he was skilled with lòhrengai. The soldiers did not. He had revealed it to them now, and that would feed rumor into the city until it blazed with the story. The witch had goaded him as Dernbrael had tried. She, however, had gotten under his skin and succeeded. He knew how, too. It was the way that she suggested he had wanted, even enjoyed killing the rogue noble. The tactic had worked because he knew, deep in his heart, that there was an element of truth to it.

He fumed quietly, trying to show none of his anger at the witch or himself. He rode to where her image had been and passed through it without hesitation. He noticed though that the soldiers did not do so. They guided their mounts to the side of the road and avoided the spot. Only the Durlin stayed with him, but they were tight-lipped and tense.

Soon, they reached the gate and passed through, the hooves of the horses loud in the gate-tunnel. He was home again. He was in Cardoroth, the city he was born in and born to rule. And his own words came back to him. *I would die for my people.*

He considered the statement. He had spoken them in anger, said them to prove that Ginsar was wrong. Were they true though? He had no way to know. Brand had proven that it was so for him. So had Shorty and Taingern. Many others had in the long history of the nation. He believed he meant it, but he was old enough to know that some things were beyond the reach of thought until circumstances arose to prove the answer one way or the other.

But those circumstances were coming. War was coming, and the Horsemen with it. Battle and sorcery. He would be tested as he never had been before. Soon, he would know the truth.

3. A Taste of Kingship

A Durlin opened the door, and Gil nodded his thanks as he entered the War Room of Cardoroth city. He had not yet washed or changed his clothes, and he felt uncomfortable walking into such a formal room covered by the dust of travel and with bloodstained bandages. But the regent had said to come swiftly, and there would be reason for that.

His steps echoed loudly. The marble floor, white and polished, was a surface that caused his boots to make a cracking sound each time the heels touched it. And the vaulted ceiling that rose to a dizzying height seemed to swallow the sound and then throw it back down at those below. The War Room was next to the Throne Room, and they shared many architectural similarities.

They were different though, too. Here, a long table of polished walnut ran dozens of feet down the length of the room. On the walls, all over them in fact, were maps. Some were very old. Some inaccurate, for they detailed far away regions more myth than reality. No one from Cardoroth had ever been to those places to verify their existence. Some were copies of maps drawn by the Halathrin. These were treasured, for the immortals had traveled widely when first they came to Alithoras, and they were extraordinary mapmakers. The majority of them, however, were of the surrounds of Cardoroth and these were the ones that would prove most useful now.

This was a room that Gil had rarely seen before. But as he stepped toward the table he had a sudden memory of his grandfather leaning over it and looking at a map that had been retrieved from the wall and spread out for study. Gil felt a stab of nostalgia. He missed him.

He stepped ahead, taking in who stood there now. Brand was at the head of the table. As always, Shorty and Taingern were nearby. Esanda was there also, and he remembered that it was she who had discovered Dernbrael's hiding place. Withholding that information in the duel had been useful. It would have irked his opponent no end not being able to find out how he had been found.

There were several other men too. Three generals and each had an adjutant. Gil approached the table and Brand's eyes flicked to him.

There was momentary concern in the man's eyes, but he covered it swiftly. Despite the blood and bandages, he realized that Gil was obviously not seriously injured. He did raise an eyebrow when he spoke though.

"I had thought there would be little trouble with fifty soldiers and the Durlin. Clearly, I was wrong. What of Dernbrael?"

Gil pulled up a chair and sat down. "To cut a long story short, he's dead."

Brand leaned back in his own chair, his expression thoughtful. "So be it. Probably for the best, I suppose."

One of the generals frowned. "You killed him? Without a trial? I cannot believe you would do such a thing."

"This is general Garling," Brand said by way of introduction.

"I think we've met, but it was some years ago. For what it's worth, I had no intention of killing Dernbrael. But he challenged me to a duel. He forced me into the fight, and so the fault is his. Had he not done so, he would still be alive."

Garling seemed less than happy with the explanation. His face reddened and he shook his head slowly. "I still cannot believe it. You did not have to accept the challenge."

"I think I did," Gil said quietly.

One of the other generals spoke. Druigbar, Gil thought his name was.

"No matter what you thought, it's a bad look. Very bad indeed. Dernbrael was a noble, no matter what crime he was accused of. He was entitled to a trial. What you have done has the appearance of an unauthorized execution."

"I agree," the third general said. Lothgern his name was, and Gil remembered that he had been sitting in the very same chair as he now was all those years ago when Gil had come in here to see his grandfather.

Gil was about to reply, but Esanda spoke first. "The nobles may see it that way, even though the man's guilt was clear. But the nobles don't count at the moment. Only the people of the realm do, and especially the soldiers. There are far graver issues to discuss."

"With respect, I *am* a noble," Lothgern said curtly. "All the generals are. And what we think counts."

Gil felt tension fill the room. But, it occurred to him that it had been like that since he entered, since before they knew about Dernbrael's death.

Esanda leaned forward and held the general's gaze. "No, you are not. You are a general in the army. Winning the battle to come is your one and only concern. In that effort, the lowliest soldier and the commanders of the army are equal, striving toward that single purpose. Nothing else counts."

None of the generals liked this, and Gil could see their tempers rising. They were about to debate the point, but Brand interrupted.

"Enough. Esanda is correct. War is coming, and we must be of one purpose. Now, nothing matters but surviving. And we have decisions to make, and swiftly if

24

we are to give ourselves the best chance. Little time remains."

"I thought we had made those decisions," Druigbar said.

Brand sat back in his chair. It was a seemingly relaxed gesture, but Gil knew him well enough to detect his frustration.

"No," the regent said, his voice matter-of-fact. "You gave your advice, and I made my suggestion. Nothing was decided."

Brand looked across the table at Gil. "Very quickly, this is the state of affairs. I tell you this now because you will be king one day, and though that hasn't happened yet, you should still have a voice in all this."

Brand rubbed his chin and gathered his thoughts. "You sent out scouts recently. They have returned, and they bring news with them. Elugs are gathering at the point where the Alith Nien spills out from the mountains of Auren Dennath. They are some thirty thousand strong, and likely to grow. With them are hundreds of Lethrin, what my people call trolls. Elùgroths have also been seen. Not Ginsar herself, as yet, but no doubt they serve her." Brand paused. "Do you follow this situation so far?"

"I do," Gil replied.

"Very well then," Brand continued. "The army is camped about one hundred and fifty miles away. That is a five day march. They will come to Cardoroth. They are not river-faring people, and no craft were seen. Therefore, the enemy will not come by water. This leaves two routes. Down the Halathrin road to the west of the river. This is a path they could travel swiftly, but it is the longer way. Or down the east side of the river, into the hills north of Cardoroth. Or, perhaps, they could split their army and do both. That is the situation we face."

Gil considered what Brand had said. He had been very brief, but all the important facts were there, including Ginsar's tactical options. The Lethrin, even in small numbers, were a great concern because they possessed enormous strength and were very hard to kill. The elugs, goblins as some people called them, were not as dangerous. But in numbers such as that, it was an enormous challenge to Cardoroth.

"We know how large the army is now, but how large could it yet grow?" Gil asked.

"That, we just don't know," Brand replied. "The mountains are full of elugs. But I suspect it will not increase much further. The scouts reported that while new elugs came down to join the army every day, that number was diminishing."

"And what fighting force can we muster? Last I heard we had twenty thousand soldiers."

Garling answered him. "It's now twenty-five thousand. Mostly foot soldiers, but we have fine cavalry also."

Gil pondered that. "And what of our food and water supplies to withstand a siege?"

"Quite adequate," Garling said. "We have masses of stored grain, for the last few seasons have been good. And our water supply has always been good. There are many deep wells within the city. They have never run dry."

"So much for us," Gil said. "But what about Ginsar? Which route will she use to reach us, and how well supplied is her army?"

Garling spoke quickly. "The elugs are not great war-makers in terms of logistics and supplies. They could not mount a long siege. Perhaps no longer than a month." He paused, looking at Brand. "As for their route, they will come down via the Halathrin road. It was built for quick-marching armies and there is no chance of ambush along its length. It's the safest, surest route and they will take it."

The other two generals were quick to agree to this, but Gil realized that this was the point of contention he had sensed earlier.

He looked at Brand. "And what route do *you* think they will take?"

"Ah, that is the question. For myself, I believe they'll come down the other way, through the hills north of the city."

"And why do you think that?"

"Because it offers the best chance of secrecy. They have great numbers, but they would still prefer to catch us by surprise, if they can. Every day of secrecy counts. They need not march to the Cardurleth itself. If they can get within a day or two before we discover them, it's still a great advantage."

Gil thought about that. It was true. They were never a chance of taking the city by storm. There was always going to be a battle. But surprise gave the advantage of being proactive to them and the disadvantage of being reactive to Cardoroth.

"There is another reason," Brand said.

"What's that?"

"The elug tribes have no love for flat and open country. They prefer hills and trees for cover. It's the type of landscape that they're used to."

Gil mulled that over as well. Much of all of this was guesswork, but that was all they would have to go on until it was too late to make a difference.

He studied the generals. He knew their type. They were cautious men, promoted because of the influence of their families. They may or may not be skilled at warfare. Sadly, promotion through the ranks of government or army officials seldom related to ability.

"Do you think the enemy may split their force and come both ways?" he asked.

"No," Garling answered. "There is no advantage in it."

"On that, we concur," Brand said. "But the reason they will see no advantage in it is because they will hope to surprise us, but surprise or not, they will expect us to wait within the city and use the Cardurleth as our defense."

"They will expect that," Druigbar said, "because it's the sensible course of action. Why should we not sit secure behind our wall?"

"Well," Brand answered, "normally you would be right. But what sort of security does the Cardurleth offer against sorcery?"

Gil could sense they were close now to the real point of difference between views. And he thought he knew what it was.

"Please go on, Brand. What do you think Ginsar will do?"

"It's not possible to know anything for certain. But this is likely. She will rely on numbers first – her army is large. Then she will turn to the Horsemen. We have seen Death and Age already. Betrayal and War are yet to come."

"We don't know that for certain," Lothgern said quietly.

Brand turned his blue eyes upon the general, and there was no doubt in them. "I do. They will come, but even they are not the greatest threat."

Brand paused. Gil knew what he was going to say next. It was his quest to solve this problem, but he had not done so yet. He had found the White Lady, and he knew that she was the key. But she could not, or would not, reveal to him what he must do.

"The Riders," Brand continued, "are summoned from another world. Ginsar has opened a gateway between the two. In the end, it is this that poses the greatest peril. There are forces within that other world that would seek dominion of ours. They are greater by far than Ginsar.

Already we are in peril of that, but should Ginsar be forced to increase the strength of the Horsemen in order to defeat us, it may open that gateway so wide that nothing could prevent their entry. The Horsemen would lead a wave of conquest across our world, and nothing could stop them."

Garling cleared his throat. "I don't know much about magic, but I fail to see how this has any real bearing on our decision."

"It's simple enough," Brand said. "The Cardurleth will keep us safe. But the enemy learned that last time. Why come again for the same purpose? I think Ginsar has a plan. It will involve the Horsemen, and their strength grows each time we meet them. She draws it into them from the other world. Where they ride, terror will follow. She will draw *more* from the other world, feeding them power. Increased in strength, and with an army, Cardoroth will fall. She will only give them enough power for them to win. But to win, she may give them greater power than she can then control. In the end, they will control her. This must be prevented at all costs."

"I see what Brand is getting at," Gil said. "The proposal is that we strike first. That we go out and meet them before Ginsar increases their power. In that way, just maybe we can prevail too quickly for Ginsar to increase their strength."

"Yes," Brand said.

The generals all seemed to object at once. Gil listened to them carefully. Their main argument was that there was just no evidence to prove any of it.

"I hear you," Gil said at length. "I hear you, but this much is true beyond doubt. The Horsemen exist. Ginsar summoned them from another world. That gateway remains open. Until it is closed, anything is possible. She can increase their strength. Perhaps even bring back the two Horsemen that have been vanquished. And Alithoras is in great danger every moment that gateway remains open. Most of all, Ginsar is insane. She would perhaps destroy the world just to beat us."

The generals remained unconvinced. For some while they spoke of the strength of the Cardurleth and the history of the city. It had never fallen to an enemy. "We believe," Garling said, "in swords and spears and arrows. And most of all, we believe in the Cardurleth and the courage of the men to hold it."

They had made up their mind, and nothing was going to change it. But Gil had been asked for his view, and he was still weighing up everything that was being discussed.

"You speak little of Ginsar," he said to the generals. "And I realize that you're familiar with battle and fighting much more so than magic. But please accept that what Brand and I say about her and the gateway is true. That being the case, do you still recommend the same defensive strategy?"

Garling leaned forward earnestly, resting his hands on the table as he spoke. "The Cardurleth is our strongest defense, no matter what. Stay here. Man the wall. Trust in our soldiers to do what they are trained for."

"And if Brand is right? That by going out to meet the enemy unexpectedly we have a chance of joining battle before Ginsar has strengthened the Horsemen? Perhaps our best and only chance to stand against the force she might otherwise unleash upon us?"

"He is *not* right," Garling said adamantly. "Nor is he right about the route the enemy will take to reach us. And if we march off into the wilderness, then we will leave Cardoroth undefended."

"That isn't so," Brand replied. "We could leave enough soldiers here to defend the Cardurleth. And our scouts will tell us soon enough if we are right or wrong about the route our enemies will take. If so, we can still return to Cardoroth in time."

Gil turned to Taingern and Shorty. "What do you two say?"

"I agree with Brand," Shorty said simply.

"And you, Taingern?"

The Durlindrath sighed. "Everything is a risk. But weighing it up, I agree with Brand too. I have seen Ginsar. She's insane and consumed by hate. She'll do what it takes, draw whatever power is necessary from the other world, to win. Sometimes offense is the best course of defense. That is the case now."

It was quite a dilemma, and Gil felt it keenly. Nothing was certain, and no strategy could be counted on to deliver perfect results. Whatever choice was made, there was risk of failure.

Brand sat calmly, though Gil guessed he did not feel that way. Nor was there any sign of anxiety when he spoke.

"Well, Gil, you have heard the arguments, for and against. I am regent. I could command, but I will not. You are a man now, and Cardoroth is your future and not mine. You must decide in this case. I will fulfill your wishes in this."

It was not what Gil was expecting. He had thought his opinion had been sought rather than a decision. But he recognized what Brand was doing. Even now, he was teaching him, allowing him a voice in the future of Cardoroth, giving him a feel of the awesome responsibility that came with leadership.

He felt the gazes of everybody upon him, waiting upon his choice. It was a taste of kingship, a taste of what it would be like to be responsible for a nation. It was too much responsibility, but it must be borne anyway. It was his duty, and it must be gotten used to.

But what choice should he make? The wrong one would lead to ruin.

4. Dust and Ash

Gil sat in thought. The large room was silent. The high-vaulted ceiling above, though airy and spacious, seemed to press down and squeeze the breath from him.

It would be easy to side with Brand, for whom he would do anything. He owed him so much that he almost felt he should. But Brand would not want that. He would want him to arrive at the best decision that he could given the information he had, and make the choice that seemed right for Cardoroth. That was where his loyalty must lie.

Carefully, he considered all the arguments. One or the other would prove correct in the end. But which?

He thought he knew.

"Very well," he said. "This much is certain. *If* Brand is right, the course of action the generals advise would see Cardoroth fall, and then no doubt Ginsar would move on to other realms. Or the Horsemen would in their own right. But Brand may be wrong. Yet, if so, our army could *still* return to Cardoroth in time to defend it."

He looked around at those in the room, meeting their gaze one by one. "And if Brand is right," he continued, "then a battle will be fought at a time and place of our own choosing. But his plan still allows us, if necessary, if circumstances are unfavorable, the option to make a tactical retreat to the city. Therefore there is nothing to be lost by following his suggestion and perhaps everything to be gained. So, that's what we'll do."

The generals glanced at each other, their expressions sullen.

"Make it so," Brand said to them. "The army is ready. We will march tomorrow, according to the ideas we discussed before Gil arrived."

The nobles and their adjutants stood. They gave the customary salutes without speaking, and then they stalked from the room.

"Not a happy bunch," Shorty said brightly after they had gone.

"They don't get paid to be happy," Esanda answered with a scowl. "They get paid to do their job."

Gil let out a long breath. "There's something else that you should know," he said.

Brand's gaze settled on him. "What? Did Dernbrael reveal anything of interest?"

"No. It wasn't Dernbrael. It was Ginsar. She appeared before us as we came back to the city. It was near the gate. But it was only an image that she cast, not her real self."

"And what did she say?" Brand asked.

"A few things, and none of them good. But what worries me is that she knew what had happened with Dernbrael. Perhaps she had a personal connection with him, and because of that link could use her scry basin to keep watch on him. I don't know. But what if she is able to use the scry basin to see us march tomorrow?"

Brand thought about that, drumming his fingers on the table. It was a rare sign of anxiousness.

"As you say, I think she had a personal connection to Dernbrael. He had likely fallen under her sway, and that made it easier. Scry magic is unpredictable. And hers all the more so. Do you understand why?"

Gil nodded. "It's not like it was for me under the Tower of Halathgar. In her case, she uses blood. That's said to give powerful results, but with even less control. Blood magic is a force of chaos."

34

"Exactly," Brand agreed. "It's a one in a thousand chance that she'll see us in time for it to make any difference."

"It's much more likely," Esanda commented, "that spies in the city will send her word. We must count on that happening, but again it's unlikely for that news to reach her in time for her to act on it."

"We can only do what we can do," Brand said. "It will have to be enough. But the seer warned me of the possibility of Ginsar using her scry basin on me or the army. She said I would sense it when it happened. I have not … not yet. And if I do, I will try to repel her."

Gil ran a hand through his hair and sighed. "There's just so much that we don't know."

"That's true," Brand answered. "But there's much that we do. For instance, we know that the elùgroths around Cardoroth have long had a hold over the elugs that dwell in the mountains north of us. Ginsar can summon them to war. But how well will they fight? They aren't well organized like the ones from the south. We have an advantage over them there."

"We know also," Shorty added, "that we gave the southern elugs, those from the Graèglin Dennath mountains, a bloody nose last time they attacked. And our scouts report no sign of them, so that allows us greater freedom to march from the city."

"We know this too," Brand said. "We'll do our best to protect Cardoroth. If we fail, it will fall. But then someone else will be next. So we must *not* fail. If we do, then the Dark will hold the south as well as the north of Alithoras, and everyone in between will be squeezed in a death grip. And as I say, we must not let that happen. We *will* not."

Gil laughed, and Brand raised an eyebrow.

"You make winning sound like an act of faith."

Brand grinned at him. "Ah, but it is. I'm not oblivious to all that could go wrong. But yes, it's an act of faith. The thought comes first and the deed follows."

It was an attitude that Gil had never been quite able to achieve. He understood that the *will* to win was a strong factor in doing so, that belief gave rise to action and that the power of the mind was greater by far than most people realized. He knew also that self-doubt was more disabling than any enemy blow. He knew all this, but even so the responsibility that they *must* win was a terrible burden. And it gave rise to the thought that they might not. Brand seemed able to ignore that. Gil could not. Failure meant that the world he knew would be turned to dust and ash. How could he put that from his mind?

5. When the Time is Right

Gil left the War Room with a troubled mind after the meeting. So much was happening so fast. But above it all, beyond strategies and preparations for war, one thing remained clear. He had been set a quest by the spirit of Carnhaina. She had charged him to close the gateway between worlds that Ginsar had opened.

He had not done so. Nor had he even discovered *how* to do so. The White Lady, however, knew what he must do. He was sure of it, but all she would say to him was that he would know what to do when the time was right.

It was time to talk to her again. With war imminent, she might reveal whatever it was that she knew. Brand had allotted her a room in the palace, quite close in fact to Gil's and the one he had given Elrika. Yet despite their proximity he seldom saw her. It was almost as though she avoided him.

He got there swiftly, walking so fast that his two Durlin guards struggled to keep up with him. Briskly, he knocked on the door.

"Come in, Gil," the White Lady said.

A shiver went up his spine. She had known it was him without looking. He decided to ignore that though. With her, it was best to just accept who she was and what she was like. To ask her questions only seemed to encourage her reticence.

"I won't be long," he told the guards.

He opened the door and stepped into her room. She was seated in a chair near the window, gazing out with a faraway look on her face. But when he entered she turned her gaze on him and smiled.

Not for the first time, Gil was amazed at the radiance of her expression and the warmth that emanated from her. She was kindness and goodness personified. But there was always something sad about her as well, and this lent her a heartbreaking beauty.

He smiled back. Brand was the only person that she really talked to, and he had a feeling that the regent understood more of her purpose than anyone else. But looking at her now, he trusted her. She was here to help, and if she would not tell him what he wanted to know, he would not, could not, hold it against her. There must be a reason. Still, he intended to press her hard for answers.

"Please have a seat," she said.

Gil pulled up a chair opposite her, and looked out the window at the city below. It was a thriving place. People filled the streets and went about their daily tasks. Did they know yet that war threatened everything they loved?

"You have come," the White Lady said softly, "to learn what you must do to close the gateway between worlds."

"Perhaps I've come just to talk to you," he answered. "You spend too much time in here by yourself."

She smiled at him once more, and there was that look again: beauty and kindness tinged with a sadness that cut deep.

"I am not of this world, Gil. I should not be here. Nor the Horsemen."

"That may be, but still you are entitled to happiness. This room is not a prison. You are free to go where you will, see what you want and enjoy Cardoroth."

She gazed out the window. "Tomorrow I will. The army will march, will it not? I will be with it."

"How do you know that, lady?"

"I know many things, Gil. I know that the enemy prepares to march against us. I know that Brand is right and that they will come down through the hills and seek to surprise us."

Gil studied her. She seemed as any young woman. Here, in her apartment, she was barefoot, one leg pulled up beneath her on the chair, and wearing a simple white dress. But there was far more to her than he knew. She held secrets within secrets and possessed power beyond his understanding.

"How is it that you know these things?"

"We all have our gifts. Everyone does, even the Horsemen. Mine, at least in this world, is to see what could be, what should be and to make the latter happen."

"What could be and what should be are far from the same thing."

"Further than you know."

Gil looked at her. There was softly spoken determination in her voice. The mystery of *what* she was drew him. But the thought of *who* she was, as a person, was stronger still.

"What is your world like, lady?"

"Ah, Gil. There's so much I could tell you. But I mustn't. The gateway should not exist. Our worlds are separate, and should stay that way. It's best that you know little."

Gil sighed. "Is that why you keep to yourself so much?"

She looked away. "It's one of the reasons. There is another." She glanced back at him. "The future will come soon enough, Gil. In the meantime, have confidence in Cardoroth. She is a strong city, filled with strong people. Ginsar and the Horsemen are as shadows. There is no joy in them. Only lust for power. And the darkness consumes them so much that they cannot see their danger. That will serve us well."

"You are speaking, I think, of how the gateway will be closed," Gil ventured.

"Yes. But please, don't ask me any more."

"I will know what to do when the time is right?"

"Yes."

"Then lady, I will leave it at that. I trust you."

She smiled at him again, and this time it was dazzling. All felt right in the world. "Thank you." She looked out the window a moment later, her expression wistful now. "You will have to make choices when the time comes. And if I tell you more now you may refuse then."

"Will they be so bad?"

She did not look at him. "You will see. But in the meantime, ponder this."

She stood and strolled to the wall nearby. Gill followed her.

There was a painting there, and she gestured at it. "Tell me what you see?"

He looked at the painting. He had seen it before, and others much like it.

"I see Carnhaina, the great queen who once ruled here. She appears much younger than she is normally depicted. She's tall and thin. With her I see her father and mother, the first king and queen of Cardoroth. That must be her younger sister there too. And I see all her brothers."

Gil fell silent. He had realized something that he had overlooked before.

"You have noticed something?" The White Lady asked.

"I suppose so. Carnhaina is famous. So too are the first Durlin. Some of them died to protect the king against assassins. I just never thought of it before, but those same Durlin were Carnhaina's brothers."

"That is so, Gil." She hesitated, as though waiting for him to say more, and then went on. "Carnhaina never had it easy. She had to make choices too, some of them dark. But she was able. You are her heir, and you will do as well as she."

Gil inclined his head. "Thank you for your confidence in me."

"And thank you for yours in me. But I think you should see someone else now."

"Who is that?"

"Elrika. She's not best pleased with you."

"Why not? What did I do?"

"Speak to her, Gil, and find out."

With a hand on his shoulder, she guided him to the door. She seemed so frail and small, but he knew there was strength in her. One day soon she would reveal her true powers.

"I'll be with the army tomorrow, when it marches," she said.

"It would be safer for you here, you know."

"I wasn't born into this world to be safe," she answered.

He said his goodbye and moved along the corridor to Elrika's room. He had barely finished knocking when the door opened. Elrika stood there, dressed in trousers and tunic with the Durlin sword at her side.

"Ah, it's you."

"Can I come in?"

"Why ask? You don't seem to consult me about anything else."

Gil hesitated. "We can fight here in the corridor if you prefer. But it won't be as comfortable."

She arched her eyebrows at him. "You've learned more from Brand than you know."

"I'll take that as a compliment."

"I suppose it is," she said. "Come in then."

He moved inside her apartment but she did not offer him a chair, nor did she sit herself.

For a moment she stared at him, taking in his bandages. "Well?" she said eventually.

"Well what?"

"I heard what happened with Dernbrael." She looked at his blood-stained dressings again. "It was quite the fight, apparently."

"It wasn't easy," he said. "For many reasons, it wasn't easy at all."

Her gaze softened, slightly. "I know that. What I don't know is why you didn't take me with you."

"There's only one reason for that. I didn't want to take you into danger. I had soldiers and Durlin with me, but I didn't know for sure that he was by himself or if he had warriors with him."

She put her hands on her hips. "Fool. How would you feel if I went into danger and didn't take you with me?"

He had no real answer for that, but he knew he would not like it. "I would feel … I don't know. I would want to help but be unable to do so."

She studied him a moment. "Exactly," she said in a softer voice. "And will you ever do that to me again?"

"I'm sorry. I didn't see it that way before. And no, I won't."

She relented then. "You could have been hurt."

"Actually, I *was* hurt."

"I meant killed. And I wouldn't have been able to do anything to stop it."

He knew what she had meant, and he knew that he would feel the same way in her position.

"Anyway," she said. "The worst didn't happen. So let's forget about it. Have a seat and tell me about it."

They sat down around a small table and he told her of how Esanda had found Dernbrael and what unfolded after that, including Ginsar's appearance.

"I still don't see why you accepted his challenge to duel," she said toward the end of his explanation.

"It was a matter of honor, partly. And what sort of king will the people think me if they also wonder if I'm a coward?"

"You worry too much about what other people think. But anyway, I can't help feeling that it was personal too. Dernbrael was trying to usurp your throne. And he tried to kill both you and Brand. That's as personal as it gets, and I think you reacted in that vein."

"Ginsar said I *wanted* to kill him. She said there was a dark side to me. Just like her."

Elrika reached out and touched his hand. "There's a dark side to all of us, but mostly we keep it under control. You did so with Dernbrael. It was *he* that sought the duel."

"Yes, but I was the one that agreed to it."

"You had reasons. They're probably even good ones."

"I suppose so. But after it was all over … I enjoyed it too."

She looked at him carefully. "Listen to me, Gil. You are *not* like Ginsar. You're nothing like her at all. Could you become so? Maybe. But so could we all. That is the lesson here. Just don't let that happen."

Gil smiled at her. She was not necessarily right, but she was trying to make him feel better. "You're a good friend."

"You just remember it! Now, you'd better get cleaned up. And let Arell change those bandages."

"I will. But there's one more thing to tell you yet."

"I'm listening."

He could tell that she was still upset with him, but he put that aside. "Cardoroth is now at war. Ginsar is

43

gathering an army of elugs from the mountains of Auren Dennath. They will soon march on us."

Elrika took the news calmly. She had been expecting it no doubt. Most people in the city did, in a vague sort of way. But it was a different thing to have your fears confirmed no matter how much you had been anticipating them.

"Are we ready for them?"

"I think so. As ready as we can be. Especially Brand. I think he's been planning for this a long time. He managed to surprise our generals too, so let's hope he can surprise Ginsar as well."

"What's his plan?"

"We're not going to wait behind the walls. We're going out to meet them, to strike first before Ginsar is ready. And before she opens the gateway between worlds any wider."

She thought about that for a moment. "Good," she said. "Best to get this over with."

"In the end, the only way to truly win this is to close the gateway."

Elrika pursed her lips. "The White Lady still won't tell you what she knows?"

"Nothing," Gil said. "She won't tell me anything at all. But I feel that I already know, at least that the answer is within my grasp, but I just can't quite see it."

"It doesn't matter Gil. Trust yourself. The answer will come eventually. And trust the White Lady. There's no harm in her. Whatever she does, whatever she says, or doesn't as the case may be, she has our best interests at heart."

Gil knew she was right. He made ready to leave, for he had to see Arell and then rest. Tomorrow would be a long day. But she placed a hand on his arm as he stood.

"Is there anything else you need to say?"

There was a glint in her eyes, and he knew this was important to her.

"Will you ride with me tomorrow when the army marches?"

"You know I will. But you may have to give me some lessons on the way. I haven't ridden much before."

"Of course. And I'll make sure you have a quiet horse."

They hugged, and he left her then. He felt rather strange, because while he would do anything to protect her he also wanted her with him. But at the same time, if something happened to her he would never forgive himself.

6. I Accept your Gift

Ginsar breathed deep of the air. It was fresh and cool and clean. She did not like it. Better by far were the pungent smells of the forest, and the shadows and sense of secrecy that went with it. But her coming here had been worth it.

The mountains of Auren Dennath climbed as a wall before her. All pine-clad slopes, twisting valleys and high ridges. It was blue too. Everything was blue from a distance except the snow-scattered ridges and the high peaks, capped by white.

She did not like the mountains. Nor the river that chattered away beside her, fed by the snows above and gushing down into the rest of Alithoras. The Alith Nien it was called in the old tongue. The Silver River. And it flowed into Alithoras, the Silver Land. She shook her head. A pox on the old tongue! Beauty was not found in nature, nor in people. It was found in power only. And *that* she had exercised in the last few days.

She had walked those blue mountains in ages past, knew the trails and the hidden valleys, knew the caves and grottoes where elugs dwelt. It had not been hard to find them again in the last few days, to draw them once more under her sway. It had been harder with the Lethrin who preferred the rocky heights, but they too were coming to war.

She cast a grim gaze over her acolytes. They liked this place no more than she. They sat and talked quietly by the river, away from her. At least down here the river slowed. It was loud and rushing no more. And this bend within it was a nice and secluded spot. The sandy shore was annoying though. But it did not run any great length. It soon gave way to a shelf of rock, and then a tree-clad hill rose to the side offering them shelter from prying eyes and something of the seclusion of the forest to which they were used.

It was sunny though, bright light everywhere. The acolytes hated that. But they were weak, even if useful at times. And she would have a special use for two of them soon. It was true though that the dark was better, but she could put up with the sunlight. Her army was coming to her, gathering nearby, and soon they would march.

Movement caught her gaze and disturbed her thoughts. One of the acolytes approached.

"He comes, Mistress."

It was just as well. She did not like this waiting. She turned her gaze up toward the hill. For a moment, she saw nothing. Then the black-clad form of her most powerful acolyte appeared from behind a stand of trees. With him were three elugs and a single Lethrin.

The small group scrambled down the steep slope. There was a trail there, of sorts, but it was a tangled mess of tree roots and loose rock. The acolyte descended clumsily. The elugs negotiated the slope with ease, though little grace. The Lethrin however, who should have fared the worse because of his size, moved with incredible nimbleness and balance.

The Lethrin, ahead now of all the others, leaped down the last of the trail to the rock shelf like a mountain deer. There he waited for the others, and his dark eyes found Ginsar and studied her.

She felt the strength of his will through that gaze. All the Lethrin were strong of body. Some of mind too, but here was a paramount individual. She could use that. Yes, he would be most fitting for what she had in mind, and the plan that she had nurtured for some while would be altered. And for the better. She smiled, but the creature gazed back at her implacably. Better and better.

The others joined him and the acolyte took the lead again. They approached her, and her heart quickened. Soon now her plan would come to fruition and her army would march.

The small group drew to a stop before her. The acolyte bowed, and the elugs followed his lead. The Lethrin merely inclined his head, the dark gaze of his deep-set eyes never leaving her own.

She turned to the acolyte. "The army is now gathered?"

"Yes, Mistress."

"And what are the final numbers?"

"We have thirty-five thousand elugs. Most of them are armed with swords, but some carry maces and timber clubs."

"And the Lethrin?"

The acolyte began to answer, but the Lethrin interrupted.

"We are one thousand strong, Ginsar. Our numbers may be few, but we are strong."

Ginsar was surprised. Most men trembled at the thought of even talking to her, and very few dared call her by her name.

She looked into his eyes. "I accept your gift."

The Lethrin gazed back, puzzled but undaunted. "What gift?"

She smiled at him. "The strength of your people. Even one … just one, is gift enough."

He did not answer that, and she read uncertainty in his expression. But she knew exactly what she meant, and he would understand soon enough.

After a moment, he inclined his head once more. But his expression remained perplexed.

She kept her face neutral, but in her heart she felt a surging thrill and the joy of life buoyed her spirit.

"Are you ready to kill?" she asked him.

"Yes."

"Are you ready to make war?"

"Yes."

"Then together we shall make war such as the race of man has never seen before!"

7. Leave the War to Us!

Gil sat on a roan mare. Elrika rode beside him on a quiet gray. Brand was nearby, and all the Durlin too, sitting proudly on their mounts and looking relaxed and yet ready to move into action at any moment. It was the look of the elite warrior, and Gil admired it.

The White Lady sat quietly on her mount, a pure white. Gil had never seen the horse before, and he was not sure where it had come from. But it was a fitting mount for her, even if unusual with its pink nose and blue eyes.

Elrika seemed calm, but he knew there were nerves beneath the surface. Yet no one had said anything about her presence, although the eyes of the Durlin strayed sometimes to her sword, the blade of that long-ago first Durlin. Gil realized why they did not say anything. It was because they respected her. She was not as skilled as they, but she was young. One day she would surpass some of them in skill, perhaps all of them. They had seen her use a blade, and they knew talent when they saw it. They accepted her as Gil's unofficial guard, and her place in the army too.

Dawn streaked the sky. Gil looked behind him. Cardoroth was awash with color, the low-glinting rays of the sun striking flashes of red from the strange stone of the city buildings. It was his home. It would always be his home. But he rode away now to protect it, if he could.

They had begun to pass through the city streets when it was still dark and the people mostly asleep. It had been quiet, but the smell of hearth-fires and baking bread was strong in the air. This was the last group to pass through.

The army had gone ahead of them, moving in regiment after regiment through the night.

"Do you think moving the army under cover of dark worked?" Gil asked Taingern as the Durlindrath neared him.

"It's hard to hide the movement of an entire army. But it had to be tried. Likely a lot of people noticed something was happening, though not necessarily what and on how big a scale."

Shorty joined the conversation. "People would have noticed, but they would have noticed a lot more if the army marched during the day with fanfares and parades. Although the men would have missed all those well-wishers and the shouts of friends and the familiar faces of their families to see them off. But it couldn't be helped. Brand was right to march as secretly as possible."

"When will the city be told?" Gil asked.

"Brand left instructions," Taingern said. "No announcement will be made until two days after we've gone."

Shorty laughed. "And then they'll be told that the army marched along the old Halathrin road, and that going to the North Gate was a ruse."

"Hopefully all these things will throw the spies off our track," Taingern said.

"Most of them anyway," Shorty agreed. "But some in the city will have noticed what's going on and made guesses. They may try to follow us, and then get word to the enemy."

Soon after, they came to the North Gate, the Harath Neben as it was properly known. Gil studied the two massive emeralds representing the constellation of Halathgar. The gate was also called Hunter's Gate, for the north road, out where the army now was, lead to wild lands of plentiful game. Gil had been through it before, but had not ever gone far into the lands beyond.

They rode on. Sunlight bathed the forested hills ahead. Behind, the city streets remained gray shadows. The road they followed ran straight at first, and then it began to swing to and fro as it climbed toward higher ground. Within half an hour they crested a hill and drew rein.

Brand sat upon his beloved black stallion, an old horse that had been his mount before he was the regent or even the Durlindrath. His hand was always reaching out to stroke its neck, but now he held the reins in a tight fist and Gil saw an emotion on his face that he had seldom seen before. Fury.

Below, gathered on a large expanse of grassland within a valley, was the army.

Gil glanced at Shorty. "What's the matter?"

"Brand instructed the generals to take the army into the hills and well beyond the city. They have not done so."

The regent nudged the stallion forward, and the group set off again. Brand had regained control of his emotion, but the look on his face was still cold and bleak.

As they moved down the slope Gil studied the army. He had never seen that many people in one place before. Twenty-five thousand men, their helms glinting, standards and flags sparking myriad colors into the air and the hope of a nation about them like an aura. This was what stood between the forces of evil and the people of Cardoroth. And he felt a sudden surge of pride that he was going to be a part of it.

The riders negotiated the slope down to the floor of the valley and passed through the outer perimeter of sentries and into the army.

Brand was in the lead, his black stallion moving with grace as though it knew it was making an entrance. Upon the regent's head was the Helm of the Duthenor, glittering silver in the early light. He sat tall and proud in the saddle, not like a regent but like a warrior-king of old.

The Halathrin blade, sheathed at his side, was no ornament and the soldiers knew it. Brand was the finest fighter in Cardoroth, if not Alithoras. There was no one they wanted with them more than him, for once upon a time he had been one of them. A soldier, a fighter. He had earned a place as a captain after a deed of unsurpassed bravery. And then surpassed it anyway to become Durlindrath.

All about him soldiers waved and yelled out to him and cheered. Brand acknowledged them, and here and there he even called to some by name. He knew these men, had served with them before his rise to power. He was, and always would be, one of them. That was why they respected him. He knew them. He cared about them. And there was a lesson in that. One that he had been teaching Gil for a long time, and one that Gil thought he had understood but now knew he was only just beginning to learn.

Thus they passed through the army, and it took much time to reach the front. Gil realized that it would have been much faster to have skirted round it than to pass through it. But Brand did nothing without reason. Why then had he done this? To help lift the morale of the men? That seemed likely enough. But also perhaps to gauge it in the first place. That seemed likely too. Or maybe to reinforce his bond with the soldiers? At some point he may fall out with the generals, especially if they disobeyed him, and he would want the support of the men. All of these seemed good reasons for what he had done. Perhaps *all* of them were right.

Unease settled over Gil. That there was a fundamental difference in view between the generals and Brand was apparent. That was no good thing, because in war the leadership of an army must send clear and unified messages to the soldiers. Doubt and discord were deadly. And Brand would certainly wish to lead the army himself, yet the generals were more experienced, and historically generals led Cardoroth's armies. The old king had been an exception. He was not the only one, but he was a rarity. This meant the generals would seek to wrest power back. The question was, what would Brand do?

At length the riders came through to the front. Brand angled his black stallion then toward where the generals were talking with their adjutants. Nearby, soldiers were saddling the generals' horses.

The anger that was in Brand resurfaced, though Gil knew he was holding it in check now, but some crept through into his voice when he spoke.

"Why have the men not marched well away from the city as I asked?"

Garling turned his gaze to the regent, and there was no give there.

"The men were tired from the long night of activity. They needed rest, and I ordered them to establish a camp here."

Brand did not back down. "You've given them a rest, and thereby increased the chances of them dying. They will not thank you."

"How so?" Garling answered. "What risk is there in this?"

"There are spies in the city. They will seek to follow us. Even now they may be in the forest, ahead of us. Nor was the gate closed as I asked."

Garling shook his head. "You imagine dangers and grow them in your mind. There may be spies. But marching from the city and closing the gate would not have stopped them."

"Perhaps not, but it would have reduced their numbers. Everything we can do to hinder them should be done."

"I considered these issues, and I made my choice."

"And the other generals?"

Druigbar answered. "We agreed with Garling. He is the most senior and most respected officer in the army."

"That, in short, is the answer to all your questions," Garling said to Brand. "We are the military experts here. We know what we are doing, and we insist that you leave the war to us. Do not interfere any further."

It went quiet. Gil knew that his earlier musings were correct. This was a power struggle, and the generals had deliberately ignored Brand's orders to force a confrontation and establish their authority at the outset.

The tension hung in the air, and Gil knew that Brand could not tolerate this. But Brand surprised him. The regent merely inclined his head.

"As you say, you are the experts. Carry on."

Garling signaled for a horn to be sounded, and the signal was given for the army to march. Brand fell back behind the generals as the army moved forward at a steady pace.

Shorty chuckled softly. "You're playing a dangerous game, Brand."

Brand gave a slight shrug, but did not comment.

"What game?" Gil asked.

"He doesn't trust the generals," Shorty said quietly. "The old king, your grandfather, was the great strategist. These men, they mostly just executed his decisions. In themselves, they're not really tested and proven." He lowered his voice still further. "Worse than that, Sandy suspects they were in league with Dernbrael, but she's not positive of the information she has. And given what we now know of Dernbrael, that means they might be in league with Ginsar. We just don't know."

That was a shock to Gil, and even Shorty seemed solemn as he spoke the words.

"So what is the game that Brand is playing?"

"Like I say," Shorty answered, "a dangerous one. It's hangman's noose. And he's giving them enough rope."

8. I have Obeyed!

Night fell, and a blanket of stars smothered the sky. The dark was to Ginsar's liking, and she became more alert, more focused, more alive.

In the distance she heard the rumblings of her army. It was massive. It would crush Cardoroth. And then who knew where it would sweep her?

She put that last thought aside. First things came first. Brand was her great enemy. It would not do to forget that, to take her mind off that battle until it was won. He had a way of surprising her, and she must not let that happen again.

The smell of smoke from thousands of cooking fires filled the air. Now that night had fallen, the ruddy glow from the army's camp lit the horizon. Ginsar liked that. Fire was better than starlight.

Tomorrow she would join the army and lead it. Cardoroth awaited them. But before that, she still had two tasks to accomplish. She was not looking forward to the first. It always drained her, and it was dangerous. But the second would be her reward for the first.

She pulled her black cloak closer about her, and drew the dark hood over her head. Slowly, silently, she summoned her power. Elùgai crept through her body, seeping out from her very bones and tingling her skin. She wrapped it about herself, cocooned herself in its embrace. The magic took on the darkness of the night. It became one with the shadows. It was the whisper of the wind in the tree tops and the bubble and lap of the river nearby.

Now that no one could see or hear her, Ginsar rose and slipped from the camp of her acolytes unnoticed. She had business of her own to attend to and questions that needed answers.

She moved toward the river and followed it downstream. It was better to be alone, away from the furtive glances of her followers and their incessant talk. Soon they were swallowed up by the night behind her. Even the distant noises of the army became more muted. At last, she was alone and one with the dark about her.

She let the elùgai that concealed her slip away. Great though her power was, she must still conserve it. It would be tested tonight, and also in the days to follow.

It grew darker. Clouds scudded across the sky. All that she could hear now was the soft murmur of the river. It ran slower here and widened out.

She came to another bend. Trees began to grow thickly, and she slipped within them like just another shadow of the night. It was black and sky-less here, the canopy of leaves a dome above her. It reminded her of a tomb, and well it might for in a way it soon would be.

Taking her time, for even her sharp eyes strained to penetrate the gloom, she moved toward the bank of the river. When she found it, she liked what she saw. It was suitable for her purpose.

The trees were willows now, and here by the edge of the river there was no shelf of rock nor margin of sand. It was an earth bank, and the hanging branches of the trees dangled out over the water.

Probing with her mind, she sensed that the river had gouged out the soil beneath the bank so that while she stood upon ground she stood over water too. That also was fitting for her purpose, because she must invoke that feeling with her magic: the feeling of different worlds in the same place, the melding of one reality with another,

58

the summoning of a spirit long dead into the realm of the living.

In the distance, an owl hooted. A sense of menace settled over the little wood in which she stood. It reminded her of home, and that comforted her. What she would attempt now was not easy. It never was, but she sensed that this time would be even harder.

She looked out over the dimly visible water. It was sluggish, barely moving, but here and there a ripple of water shimmered and gleamed in the inky blackness.

Ginsar remembered her childhood. He that she would now summon came to her first then. Her family did not like him. But she knew better. Her sister learned from him, but she pulled away at the end. But Ginsar kept going and the secrets of the universe, one by one, became hers. Yet he, the paramount elùgroth ever to walk Alithoras, was dead.

But not to her. Even dead, she could speak to him, and she would do so now to learn of the future.

She stepped forward to the very edge of the bank on which she stood. It was now the middle of the night, that crux of time where the night was neither young nor yet old. It was a moment in between, a transition of what was into what would be.

The willows moved behind her, their whip-like branches trailing like long and skeletal fingers probing the dark air. The water before her began to toss restlessly. A glimmer of starlight lit the river, but it touched only the surface. The murk below was impenetrable. Except to her magic, and she summoned it now, drew it in from the world about her.

Ginsar stood to her full height. Out, out her mind spread, casting tendrils of thought over the water. And then she plumbed the murky depths, becoming one with it, feeling its currents and then sinking lower until her mind perceived the mud-slicked bottom.

Unease gripped her once more. It always did at this point, but fortune favored the fearless and she stood even straighter. She turned her magic to what must come next, and mouthed words of power that filled the air and then sank like daggers of thought into the water. Words, magic and thought were one, and they came up against the forces of nature that held the world together.

Fire spurted beneath the water. Her sense of unease redoubled, but she suppressed it. She made a stabbing motion with her hands, and the fire plunged into the depths of the river, deep down to the muddy bottom and the solid earth beneath.

The world grew still. A great chill descended. The stars glittered through gaps in the scudding clouds, and frost began to glisten on the narrow leaves of the willows.

Something stirred in the water. The river began to seethe. A hiss of steam escaped the surface, and then the water boiled and thrashed angrily. It writhed with forces seeking escape, forces that she had called into being. The river twisted like a live thing seeking to throw itself out of the two banks that hemmed it in.

The noise began now, as she knew it would, as it always did. It was not the splash of water nor the hiss of steam. It was desolate wailing. And on the edge of her understanding were words – bitter, angry, pleading. Above it all was a sense of threat, that she too would join the maelstrom of lost voices one day.

Then the faces began. The fire-lit water showed them all. Staring faces. Cruel faces. Kind faces. They tried to rise into the air and escape the water, but the river threw up a plume of water that slapped them all back down to the netherworld.

Ginsar stabbed again with her hands, and then she clawed at the air. A heaving vortex grew in the middle of the river. From this a figure rose, tall and majestic, robed in fiery water and crowned by white froth.

Power thickened the air, and the figure, mantled in awe and dread grandeur, drew breath and lifted high its arms. "I have come," it boomed.

The water of the river stilled its thrashing.

"Welcome, Master." Ginsar said. But her throat was dry and her words raspy. The chill about her was like ice and her breath steamed. She forced air into her lungs and spoke again. "I have summoned you because—"

"I know why you have called me. The dead see many things. In death, there is no time. What was, what is and what yet may be are all one. Speak, and I will answer. Perhaps."

This was not quite what Ginsar expected. Had she performed the ritual wrongly, made some slight error? No, she knew she had not. What then was different? She must think on that later. Maybe she was different herself.

Her unease heightened, but she forced her words out with strength this time.

"Fate hastens. War looms. The fall of Cardoroth draws nigh. What plan has Brand set in motion to try to avert the disaster?"

The shade of her Master, the long-dead spirit of Shurilgar, tilted his cowled head. She saw no eyes, nor any face, but she sensed the force of his will.

"Brand is now beyond your reach. Your chance to destroy him has come and gone. You failed, and the opportunity will not come again."

Shurilgar's voice carried over the water to her, flew into her mind like arrows. They made her heart flutter in her chest and stabbed at her like little daggers of fear. But her Master was not finished.

61

"Beware! Brand is less your enemy than you think. You have others, and, perhaps, greater. But know this also. Though Brand will not fall to you, Cardoroth yet may. Or it may not. Should you draw too deep of the world from which you summoned the Horsemen, then they shall consume you. But if you do not draw enough then you shall surely fail. Again."

Ginsar felt the cold seep into her bones, and this time the judgement of her Master was plain. And it stung her.

"I control the Horsemen. They do my bidding. Mine is the greater strength, and I do not fear them. What else should I know of my enemies?"

Shurilgar spoke again. His voice was the whisper of death, and there was a glimmer of cold eyes within the shadow of his cowl.

"Pride is a friend to some, and an enemy to others. But you should fear also the girl-child for she will stymie you, and the quiet-one who shall have his day in the sun. Yet in the end, all will hinge on the princeling. He is the key, and the past will rise to call him, and the Pale Lady shall fall at his feet, and in dying save him."

Ginsar locked those words into her memory. They made no sense, for the dead spoke in riddles. But there would be truth in them nonetheless, once she unraveled their meaning.

"And what else, O Master?"

An otherworldly breeze ruffled Shurilgar's hood, yet no such breeze touched Ginsar.

"Time slips away," he said. "Brand is not the great foe that you imagine, but he is implacable. You seek to defeat him, but all the while he plans and moves to defeat you."

Ginsar considered that. She did not yet know what the other warnings meant, but this at least seemed clear enough. Brand sought to bring the war to her instead of the other way around.

Shurilgar continued. "All hangs in the balance, child of the Dark. What was will be again, and truths long hidden will surface. They may help your cause, or hinder them."

"Then help me, O Master. Reach forth and lend me of your strength."

"The dead do not help the living."

"That is not so! Carnhaina helps Gil. Do you love me less than she loves him?"

The water of the river churned, and it seemed that the current turned and flowed upstream. Fish leapt above the surface as though trying to escape the river, but then sank without trace.

Ginsar knew she had gone too far. Summoning the dead required a perfect balance of ritual and magic. She had disrupted that. Perhaps from the beginning, but she had tipped the balance now. To invoke emotion in a spirit was a dangerous, dangerous thing to do.

Shurilgar towered above her as an angry image. Strange lights gleamed and flitted below the river surface. The water lapped the bank and tore at the solid ground. His shadow grew massive, and then he strode across the water toward her.

His hand shot out. The river heaved. His cold fingers gripped her throat, or a lash of water struck her. She felt it being forced down and into her lungs. Or maybe it was the spirit-hand of Shurilgar choking her, depriving her of air.

She tasted death. Cold, lifeless, dark and dim with the memory of the light that was.

Shurilgar spoke, and she felt the breath of his voice upon her face, unless it was instead some stirring of a breeze through the ice-cold air.

"There, princess, I have obeyed! I have obeyed! I have given you a gift. It is inside you and will help ere the end."

He cast her back and she stumbled and fell. His shadow withdrew, growing smaller, fainter as it reached the center of the lake. There it descended.

He was gone. A plume of water geysered high into the air and then collapsed again. The stench of the muddy river bottom floated through the air.

Ginsar was colder than ice. She knew she was on the threshold of death. She could not stand, for there was no strength in her legs and her mind swam. But she had use of magic, and she invoked it now.

Elùgai flared to life. It glittered at her fingers and she cast it at the willow trees. At first only the leaves caught, but then she drew deep of herself and sent a bolt of sorcery at the nearest trunk. There was a boom of thunder and the earth trembled. When that subsided, and the smoke began to clear, she saw that the trunk had started to burn, and soon a roaring fire engulfed it. This spread from branch to branch and tree to tree until the entire grove was afire.

Gradually, warmth and life returned. Never before had she been so close to death, but having survived, a wild thrill ran through her. She dared things none other did. She had power that no one else had. She would achieve that which had proven beyond her innumerable predecessors – the subjugation of all Alithoras!

She rose to her feet, and weakness washed over her. But it would pass. She knew that she had gone too far, but it would serve her well. She had angered the dead, which most would say was unwise. But Shurilgar had given her a gift in the end. He had done something, though she knew not what.

She took a few deep breaths, loving the smell of smoke about her. The warmth was seeping through to her bones, and that was a feeling of unsurpassed bliss. Never had she been so cold before.

Wrapping her cloak tightly about her, she retraced her steps back toward the camp. She could not tell what Shurilgar had done, but she felt different. No matter. His gift would reveal itself in time.

9. A Dangerous Path

The road the army followed was of ancient construction. Gil marveled at how well it had survived the millennia, for it must have been built by the Letharn during that long-ago time when their empire spanned much of Alithoras.

Yet it was not paved, but rather made of hardened earth that now grew grass. Over the long years since the demise of the Letharn others had turned it to their own purposes, keeping it relatively clear of shrubs and trees. Now, it was mostly used by hunters and woodcutters from Cardoroth.

Gil could not help but wonder why the Letharn had built it. It led to Cardoroth, but so far as he knew there were no towns or ruins or signs of habitation in this place when his ancestors founded the city. Had the Letharn come, perhaps, merely for the scry basin beneath the Tower of Halathgar that was subsequently built over it? It was possible, though he felt there was something more. Whatever that something was, it appeared to be lost in the deeps of time.

The road, according to Brand, deteriorated through the hills. This was because it saw less use. Nor was it especially wide, allowing the men to only march four abreast. This was a concern, for later, especially when they penetrated deep into the well-forested hills, the army would be strung out and vulnerable to attack. But this could not be helped, nor was it unprecedented. Still, Gil could see why the generals did not like the idea. They had mentioned it at the very start of the march, and Garling had dropped back to ride next to Brand to point it out again.

"It is exactly as we feared," the general said. "The road deteriorates swiftly, and the army will be in greater jeopardy the further we proceed."

"This is no surprise, Garling. We knew this in Cardoroth. But the swifter we travel the less our risk. Ginsar must know where we are in order to attack us."

"Perhaps so, but we should not have come here. We should return."

Brand shook his head. "It's too late now. For better or worse we're committed. To turn back would shatter the morale of the men, and they would have no respect for the army leadership. Nothing would lose us the battle with Ginsar swifter than that."

"What you say may be true, but there are limits. We don't know how much this road deteriorates. We don't know if the army can even traverse it all the way. Our maps become less accurate half way through the hills."

Brand raised an eyebrow. "You and the other generals have never been here yourselves?"

"No," Garling said.

Gil could see that Brand was surprised. The generals, more than anyone else, should be familiar with the countryside surrounding Cardoroth in all directions.

"Well, I have," Brand told the general. "The road is narrow, but it does not get narrower than it is here, nor does it deteriorate much more than this. It runs all the way through the hills and comes out the other side. There is danger in its narrowness, and in the concealment offered by hill and tree, but the remedy to that is swift marching and preparedness. The scouts will scour the area around us night and day."

"It's not the same," Garling argued. "No matter how good the scouts are they may miss something. There's just too much concealment available for our enemies."

"No, the risk cannot be entirely eliminated."

Garling did not seem best pleased, but he argued no further. "Very well, I'll send out the scouts."

Brand seemed dumbstruck. "You mean that you haven't already?"

"No. We're still close to home."

"Well, if it were me, I'd send them out now. Every one of them. And not just ahead and to our flanks but behind also."

"Their numbers are limited," Garling said. "Why behind us too? Ginsar can only be ahead of us, assuming she comes this way at all."

"Because we may be followed from the city. And then word sent ahead of us by swift rider."

Again, Garling did not argue the point, but he did not seem entirely convinced. He nudged his mount ahead and rode up to the other two generals. Brand never took his gaze off him, and the regent seemed less than happy.

The army moved deeper into the hills. There was a brooding sense about them, a feeling of an ancient land that seldom saw the movements of people and tolerated it less. The wilderness often felt that way to Gil, but it was a feeling only. It came from spending too much time walking city streets and sleeping in beds and having decorated ceilings keep off the rain at night.

Every hour the generals called a halt and the men rested briefly. They were setting a good pace, but there was a long way to go. Frequently, Brand dismounted and walked his horse. When he did so, the Durlin did likewise. Gil followed suit, but he was not sure what purpose it served. Then he understood. Partly, it was to rest the horse. Partly, it was to obtain exercise. And it was also to stay limber and combat ready. Brand did not expect trouble yet, but it was in his nature to always be prepared for it.

The trees grew more thickly, and there was little evidence of logging. Mostly there were oaks, and the trunks were gnarled and the height of the tree stunted by virtue of the rocky soil of the hills. There were other broadleaf trees too, and here and there taller pines. It was the kind of place that Gil might eventually like if he spent enough time here. Evidently, the hunters who came to this region did. Certainly, there was a sense of peacefulness and tranquility that did not exist in the city.

So the day passed. Little happened, save for the grind of the march. Well before dusk they stopped. It took time to establish a camp, dig latrines, start fires, erect tents and cook food. All of this needed to be done while daylight lasted.

Gil picketed his horse when they stopped and rubbed the roan down. Looking back, he saw that many small camps were established, and the army stretched out at least a mile behind him. It was one thing to talk about the vulnerability of an army forced to march in this fashion, but another to see it. An attacking enemy could cause great destruction. But even as he watched, sentries moved out from the long line of the army, and closer to the camp armed men stood forward to form a protective guard.

When they were done with their horses Brand approached.

"Come with me," he said, signaling both Gil and Elrika.

They moved out of their own camp, but Gil noticed soldiers coming up to form a guard at the front of the army. This was in addition to the protection already offered by a contingent of cavalry that formed a vanguard.

"Where are we going?" Elrika asked.

"I have to see someone. And it'll be educational for you both to come along. Best pull up your hoods."

Gil grinned. That was so like Brand. He rarely answered a direct question, preferring instead for people to draw their own conclusions. He had no doubt that whatever lay ahead would be interesting though, and educational. Brand, though sometimes enigmatic, did nothing to no purpose.

They melted into the army, merging with the throng of people. Brand had left his helm with the Durlin, and he seemed just an ordinary soldier. Gil and Elrika passed as the same, though less assured of themselves.

It was a long walk, for evidently they were heading to the rear of the army. And that was some considerable distance. Nor was it an easy walk, for everywhere there were moving people and cooking fires and groups of boisterous soldiers talking. They had to weave in and out of the great mass.

Eventually, they came to their destination. At the rear was the main concentration of cavalry, and also wagons full of supplies and food. These were all heavily guarded.

At the very back was a group of scouts. Brand saw them and swung in their direction. Even as Gil watched, some men went out to the flanks of the army and disappeared into the trees. Others were returning.

Brand approached a small fire where a lone man sat, his bow beside him. His companions had just left him.

"Is there a seat here for a few hungry soldiers?" Brand asked.

"By all means," the lone man replied. But even as he spoke his gaze was fixed hard on Brand's face, trying to see beneath the hood. Brand pulled it back, revealing himself for a moment, and then he pulled the hood back up.

"Well met, old friend," the regent said.

The lone man stuck out his hand, and Brand took it in the warrior's grip. "It's good to see you."

"And you," the man answered. "But I take it you're just a soldier tonight?"

"Exactly so," Brand said. "Just a soldier. And here are two more."

They all shook hands. "This is Tainrik," Brand advised.

The man had a firm handgrip and an easy smile. Gil liked him, but he followed Brand's lead and offered no name. The man guessed it anyway.

"I'm in privileged company tonight," he said. "Forgive me for not bowing, but I guess you don't wish that."

"You always were clever," Brand smiled.

"I don't think so. If I were clever I'd be away from all this and somewhere in the woods hunting deer and building a supply of food to last me the winter."

"Ah, but you'd be bored then."

"Maybe. Maybe not. Can I offer you all some food?"

"That would be nice. It's been a long day."

Tainrik collected some wooden bowls and spoons from a central area and returned to the fire. An iron pot was set against the coals to the side of the flames. From this he spooned out what looked to be stew.

"No palace meals here, I'm afraid. Just dried meat and vegetables."

"We've eaten worse," Brand said. "And a day of marching whets the appetite like nothing else."

Gil took the bowl handed to him and thanked the man. The food did not look appealing, yet when he tasted it he found it flavorful.

They ate in companionable silence for a while. All about them men were doing the same though some groups were quite loud. Tainrik was a quiet man, however.

He was obviously a scout judging from his clothing and sword. These were different from standard army issue.

Just as scouts were a different breed of men. According to what Gil had heard they tended to be loners, more at home wandering the wild lands than in company. He believed it, but he also sensed there was much more to this man than what he seemed on the surface. If nothing else, Brand's friendship with him proved it. The regent had a way of finding extraordinary people.

Brand scraped the last bit of food from his bowl. "So, what orders do the scouts have?"

Tainrik shrugged. "Just the usual. Wander around. Check things out. Then return and report what was seen to our commanders."

"And what if you discover people following us from the city?"

"Ah, I see. We were told to leave them alone unless they presented any hostile intent."

Brand shook his head in disgust. "Those orders aren't good enough. If we're being followed, the scouts should get help and bring those men in. I want to know who they are and why they're following us. These people could just be curious. But more likely they're spies. We couldn't ask for a better chance to discover who our enemies are."

Gil put down his bowl. "How could the generals not realize that?"

Brand hesitated. "Perhaps they did. They may not *want* the spies caught. It's possible."

Gil felt suddenly afraid. If they could not trust their own generals, who could they trust?

"You know your history, lad. It's been done before. Generals have betrayed their kings and their people."

Gil knew it was so. It was a discomfiting thought.

Brand stood, and everyone else got up too. He shook Tainrik's hand. "I'm sorry I can't stay longer. I have much to do tonight."

Tainrik shook the regent's hand warmly. "It's no problem. I can have a look out there," he gestured vaguely to the rear, "but what exactly do you want me to do?" He gestured in the direction of Cardoroth.

"Don't disobey your orders. But if you find we're being followed, bring word to me. I'll sort it out with the generals after that."

They shook hands, and then Tainrik turned to Gil. He hesitated, and Gil thrust out his own hand. "Be careful out there."

"Always," the man answered.

Elrika gave him her hand, but before he even gripped it he spoke. "A pleasure, my lady. I hear you're very good with that sword. Best stay close to your friend. Not all our enemies are out there." He pointed out into the forest once more.

"That's my intention," Elrika said. "I'll be ready if they come."

"I know it," Tainrik replied. He bent down and retrieved his bow.

"You always did keep your ear to the ground," Brand said. "Nothing much escapes you."

Tainrik winked at him. "I'll tell you what I find out there behind us. It shouldn't take long."

With a grin and a wave he strode off. In moments, he had slipped into the trees and disappeared into the night. They watched him go, wondering what it would be like out there. If the army was being followed, would he find the spies? That would be dangerous. But he seemed sure of his skills and confident, and that would lessen his risk.

"How did he know who I was?" Elrika asked.

Brand flashed her a smile. "Your fame grows, young lady. You saved Gil's life. The Durlin saw it, and word has spread. Tainrik is a quiet man, but a good one. He knew who you were from the beginning. Like I say, he keeps his ear to the ground."

They moved off themselves. "Going back will take much longer than coming here," Brand said. But he did not say why.

10. Into the Dark

Tainrik eased into the dark of the trees. The forest grew thick about him, but he was in no hurry to venture further into it.

A pause would allow him to grow accustomed to the dim light. It would let him become attuned to the different environment, and a different way of moving. Most of all, he had to change his thought patterns. In the wilderness, he must think less like a man and more like an animal, for the wild was a perilous place. And the most dangerous predators hunted on two legs.

For all the dangers, this was where he loved to be. Alone. Just him and the forest. There was peace and quiet here, and things followed laws and behaviors that he understood. Once you knew it, it was predictable. The city was not like that. People were not like that. And for all its peril, the forest was a safer place than the city. If you knew what you were doing.

He eased forward a hundred paces or so, and came to a stop again. He looked about him. He smelled the air. He listened to the forest noises. There was nothing out of place. Everything was as it should be, and best of all there were no people. And treasure of treasures, out here he had no supervisor. He moved when he wanted to move. He made his own choices. He was his own master. What could be better than that?

The feel of forest seeped into him, and he became one with it. Just another creature beneath its canopy, another still shadow in the dark. But he was a man, and that meant he was a hunter. And it was time for the hunt to begin.

He moved ahead, treading softly on doe-skin boots. They were quieter than regular boots, and more comfortable. The sword at his side was thin and light. Walking with it would not tire him. The bow, also small and light, was his weapon of choice. Though if he needed it, that meant that his primary skill of stealth had failed. The knives he carried were throwing knives. They too were meant for use only if stealth and arrow had let him down.

That had never happened. Yet.

He thought as he moved ahead. The forest was good for that. The senses remained alert, but the mind was free to ponder. He was no warrior. He was what he always wanted to be. A scout. And who would want to be anything else? Growing up he had heard of the fabled Raithlin scouts of Esgallien. Stories of them were legion, and he had devoured them all.

There was no one in Cardoroth who could match the Raithlin. No one even got close. He knew he did not himself, and he was the best that Cardoroth had produced. Not that he was in charge of the other scouts. Probably he did not want to be anyway. It would prevent him doing what he loved the most, which was getting out into the wild. Their leader knew little about scouting, and he stayed in the city, or the army at present, and filtered reports.

Tainrik smiled in the dark. Typical of the army, or any government institution, to put someone in charge who did not understand the issues and that had never done the work. But in this case, he did not mind. What they had done for him though was make him a captain. It was a reward for his services, and it meant greater pay for doing the same job. He was not sure, would never know for certain, but he suspected Brand had arranged that for him. Another reason to like the man.

He had done a loop through the forest, adjusting to the environment, but now he had come back to where he wanted to be. He glimpsed the road the army was following through a gap in the trees. Now that he knew exactly where it was again, he must avoid it. He moved further back into the trees and followed a parallel course. Should spies be following the army, they would not be traveling the road where they could be seen. They would be near it like him, but not on it.

Now, he must put himself in their minds. How would they be thinking? What would they do? In this way he would best be able to find them, assuming they were there at all.

This much he knew. They would hang back. It was too dangerous to follow closely to the army, and it could easily be followed from a distance. It could not hide. The chance of discovery was higher up close because there were more scouts per square mile. The further away they were, their chances of discovery lessened exponentially.

But what was *too* far away? They would need to be in striking distance if they wished to observe what was happening, if they intended sabotage, or if they intended to send word ahead of them to allies. Time was precious. Therefore, the optimum distance to trail the army was in a range of two to five miles. If it were him, he would do so at two miles, but then he was skilled at staying hidden. Were any potential spies similarly skilled? There was no answer to that, but he must assume they might be. Or if not, that they were reckless, or bold enough, to do so anyway.

He was not yet far enough behind the army to be within the likely range. He slowed though, taking greater care to move silently, and even within the dark to move from areas of deepest shadow to deepest shadow.

He must keep putting himself in their mind. That was the paramount skill of trackers. Following a trail required great expertise, but there were times that no discernable trail existed. Yet trackers could still follow their target. This was because they empathized with their quarry, understood what they would do and why.

Tainrik drew to a stop. Doing so would enable him to hear, and to smell better. It also made his movement through the forest less predictable. He never moved at the same speed nor the exact same direction for long.

Would any followers light a fire? He smelled no trace of smoke. Nor did he see the flicker of light. Of course, he would have to be close to see it. But the question was, would they light one?

No one liked eating cold food. Especially night after night. But the fear of discovery would motivate them to take less risk. Nor was it so cold, even at night, that they needed one for warmth. Yet again, if they were skilled in the wild, there were ways to conceal not only the light from a fire but also the smoke.

If they were some distance from the army, and had located a hollow, they might be confident that a fire would not be seen and the chances of someone stumbling across it by accident were very low. But what about the smell of smoke? They might risk that. It took great skill to detect the origin of a smell at night. In still air, as it was now, the smell would be faint but spread out over a large distance. And the smell could be minimized too. Old and dry timber burned cleanly.

The night began to pass. He walked forward again, keenly alert to all his senses. It was quiet. Nevertheless, a sense of unease settled over him. It was nothing more than a whisper of doubt at first, but it grew. Nor could he identify its source. He had learned to pay attention to his instincts though, and it gave him pause for thought. What should he do next?

He moved slowly now, no more than a few soft paces at a time before stopping near a tree trunk and assessing the night again. Something was disturbing him, and that he did not know what it was annoyed him. Worse, it was dangerous.

He stepped forward again, only to go perfectly still, his foot hovering above the ground. Slowly, he drew breath, turning his head gently one way and then the other. Then he had it. Smoke. He knew now what disturbed him, and for all that his body was still his heart raced in his chest.

He realized that he had been smelling the smoke for some while. It was so faint, its build up so gradual, that he had not consciously noticed. Then he heard a noise.

Gently, he lowered his foot to the ground and pulled his bowstring from a small pocket in his tunic. The noise was not close, and he risked stringing the bow. It was not good for the weapon to be strung for long periods, but now was the time to do it before it was too late.

He had not quite finished when he identified the noise. Horses. Coming close. There were riders on the road, perhaps a dozen of them.

His bow strung, he moved quietly again. It was not far to a vantage point where he could see the road the army had traveled earlier that day. Peering through foliage and trunks he saw the riders. They were a cavalry unit from Cardoroth's army. No doubt they were patrolling the road.

They rode on and the sound of the hooves diminished. But the riders had not lit any fire. The smoke was not of their doing, and it had been too faint for them to detect. Whoever had started it was still out there. Somewhere.

Not only was the person, or persons, who had lit the fire still out there, but now they would be doubly alert. The sound of the riders would have woken even a sleeping man, and no man in the forest, traveling in the wake of an army, slept deeply.

It was time to remain still and work his way through the problem. He must do something next, but what? Retreat was not an option. Brand would need to know more than this. Whoever was out there could be mere hunters or foresters.

The wind was coming from the east, but the movement of air was so slow as to barely exist. But it was enough. He was on the west side of the road, and he knew what he would likely have to do next but did not like it.

Carefully, he moved through the trees. He was trying to sense if the smell of smoke increased or diminished by heading south. It did not, and that meant that the smoke was coming from either east or west. Given the wind direction, it must be east.

He moved to the verge of the trees and studied the open road. He would have to cross it. It was dark, but he would be seen if anyone watched. Probably, whoever had lit the fire was well back from the road, but there could be more than one person. Or whoever it was could have slipped out toward the road to study the riders as they went through. He could not know, and he could not wait. The night would not last forever, and what he would have to do after crossing would take time.

There was no movement nor any sound. There was no sign of another human presence, so he stepped out of the trees and onto the road. Movement attracted the eye, so it was best to go slowly. Yet the longer he was in the open, the greater the chance of his being observed. So, he opted for a normal walk, neither fast nor slow.

Soundlessly, he crossed. But the moment he reached the cover of trees on the other side he came to a stop and listened.

The forest did not change. There was no noise or indication of movement that he could detect, no sense that anyone had seen him and fled, or headed in his direction. So far so good.

Patience was his friend now, and hastiness could get him killed. Slowly, he moved east into the breeze. He moved for some time, easing through the forest soundlessly and slipping from one shadow to the next. In time, the smell of smoke disappeared. He had overshot the camp and the breeze was taking the smoke away from him. This was confirmation that crossing the road had been correct, but it gave no indication of whether the fire was to the north or south.

There was no way to know, but he felt that the forest was thicker to the north, that it offered better concealment in that direction. If so, that would be where he would have established his camp.

He turned back, but was careful not to retrace his earlier steps. In a little while, he scented smoke again, and then turned north.

Soon, the smell of smoke became stronger, stronger than it had been at any time since he first smelled it. His choice had been correct. He slowed down even more. He noticed too that the ground became rougher and started to slope downward. That meant that there was probably some kind of hollow or gulley ahead. A likely spot to conceal a camp.

Tainrik came to a stop. His heart pounded in his chest and a cold sweat began to slick his skin. This was it. Somewhere ahead was the camp.

Was there just one man there? Were there several? Were they spies or foresters or hunters?

There was no way to know. But it was his job to find out. He ran his fingers over his bow, feeling that the string was properly attached. He adjusted the quiver on his back and counted his arrows. Twenty-one. He felt the hilt of his sword for reassurance, and then, with great care, he began to move again.

He would need all the skill he possessed, all the patience he could muster, and perhaps a bit of luck.

11. I Choose Infamy

It had taken a long time for Brand to return to the front of the army. After a little while, he had removed his hood so that he was recognized. Many spoke with him, and it seemed to Gil that he knew half the army by name. Even those he did not know, he soon turned into friends.

More than that, Gil knew, they were turned into his own friends also, for Gil had removed his own hood. Brand had winked at him when he did it, and he knew that this was the purpose for which he had been brought. He might be the Prince of Cardoroth, but he would not be seen as remote and aloof like the generals. Brand was making him one with the soldiers, as was he.

Gil relished it. These were good men, if boisterous and irreverent. But that was just how soldiers dealt with fear, and Gil enjoyed it. Here, among them, he was no prince but just a soldier. And that was a title they respected more than any royal designation.

Elrika took down her own hood too, and Gil was surprised how well she got on with the soldiers. She did naturally what he had learned from Brand.

But it was a long night, and though Gil had slept soundly, it seemed that he had barely closed his eyes before the dawn came and the army commenced to march again.

Gil walked his roan beside Brand, and he noticed that the regent seemed preoccupied.

"Is something the matter?" he asked. "You seem troubled."

Brand cast a glance back over the army that trailed behind.

"No, nothing is the matter. I've had no word yet from Tainrik is all, but it's probably too early to expect anything."

Gil understood then. Brand had sent a man into possible danger, and he did not like doing so. That it was necessary was obvious, but that did not make it more agreeable.

The morning passed. Clouds drifted in from the east, growing thicker hour by hour. The army reflected Brand's mood and became subdued, for the possibility of rain was not a good prospect. Nothing was hated more by an army on a long march, except arriving at its destination and facing battle.

The mood turned worse, for the threat of the clouds was delivered. It began to drizzle, very light but unceasing. Quickly, everything became wet, from the slippery grass the men must now tread to all their clothes and equipment.

"It's going to get worse soon," Shorty said.

He was proved correct. Soon it rained in earnest. Sheets fell in waves, turning the ground to mud.

Garling approached Brand, the other two generals behind him. "We're going to call a halt," he said.

Brand seemed furious, but he hid it well. "Halting the men in rain is no improvement on walking through it," he said.

Garling stiffened, but Taingern intervened. "Neither marching nor camping is pleasant in the rain. But there's another consideration."

"What's that?" Garling asked crisply.

Taingern seemed oblivious to his tone. "I used to hunt these parts. The terrain changes rapidly here, and the road traverses ridges and gulleys before it climbs higher in the hills and reaches a plateau. Your suggestion, general, is wise. But if the rain keeps up, which it looks like it might, we could be cut off from going forward or back, perhaps for a day or two. Yet the plateau isn't that far away. If we reached it, then we can camp, and the ground would be less muddy too."

Garling considered that. He looked like he was going to disagree, then he shrugged and nudged his horse forward.

The march continued, and Gil saw that Shorty gave his friend a sly look.

"I never knew you were big on hunting?"

Taingern looked at him, the faintest grin on his face. "There's lots of things you don't know about me."

"Aye. You're right. Until now I didn't know you could lie with a straight face. No wonder I keep losing to you when we play dice."

Taingern grinned in earnest. "I'm good with maps too, and I studied them well before we left Cardoroth. Turned out to be a good idea."

"A *very* good one," Brand said. "Thank you. But what you said about getting cut off was right."

"I know," Taingern said. "And Garling realized it too. But he would not have changed his decision on your word."

"No, that he would not. Thank you again."

They went onward, but Gil could see that Brand remained agitated. That was not like him. He always gave an air of calm confidence.

"Something is troubling you, Brand. What is it?"

The regent sighed and seemed to relax a little. "Everything we are doing is dangerous. But not acting is dangerous too. I know these hills and these forests, though my memory is dim. Armies can hide here. I don't think Ginsar's army is yet close. But each day that grows less certain. And hers is not the only army. Hvargil is somewhere outside Cardoroth. He doesn't have a proper army, but even a few hundred outlaws could pose problems in such a place as this. Severe problems. And it's often postulated that his hideout may be somewhere in these very hills."

Gil considered that. The generals may be loyal, though possibly incompetent. But if not loyal, then they may be aligned with the group of nobles that Dernbrael led. Or they may be in league with Ginsar. And now, possibly, they could conspire with Hvargil. There were too many mysteries, too many unknowns, and each was dangerous. No wonder Brand seemed anxious.

Gil considered what chance Hvargil would have of claiming the throne. It was an impossible question. He was hated by many as a traitor. But he was brother to the last king Cardoroth had. He was popular too among many of the nobles. It was all a tangled web and there were no answers. But Brand was right. To do something, anything was dangerous. Yet doing nothing was far more dangerous still. And should they defeat Ginsar, the other problems would fall away.

They moved up a steep slope, and the rain eased momentarily. Gil remained deep in thought, but he listened when Elrika asked a question.

"Brand, would you tell me something of the history of the sword Gil gave me? I know the basics, but I feel that I should learn more."

The regent guided his black stallion a little closer to her gray. "Ah, I think I know what you mean. It was like that for me too. I own a sword that great men carried before me. I knew the history as well, but I wanted to know the *people* who carried it. Is that not how it is with you?"

She looked at him earnestly. "That's exactly how it is."

"Then I shall tell you what I know, but it was long ago and, in truth, very little is remembered. Most of what I can tell you will only be the dry facts, but you will glean something of the true person who carried the sword from them."

The regent paused a moment, finding the right place to begin. Then he spoke softly, using not his voice of command and authority, but his storyteller's voice.

"Long ago, the first king of Cardoroth had many enemies. It was much then as it is today. His seven sons were the first bodyguards, the first Durlin. They were strong men, and athletic, and ever they excelled at sports and the arts of the warrior. They were tall men and lithe, and in all this they took after their father."

The regent's gaze fell to Gil. "But magic was also a part of their lineage. This came from their mother, and their mother's mother before, and on into the deeps of time that the Camar now call the Age of Heroes. It mostly bore seed in the female descendants, but not always. Whether all the seven brothers possessed magic, I do not know. But one did, and the sisters. The older sister was Carnhaina, she who afterward became the famous queen of Cardoroth. The younger sister, Ginhaina, possessed it also. In the mysteries of magic they had a tutor. What name he used, I do not know, but his true name was Shurilgar, even that same Shurilgar who was known as the Betrayer of Nations and was a sorcerer of unsurpassed power."

Brand paused. The rain increased and began to whip at them, and the horses dropped their heads and plodded on.

"Shurilgar subverted them. The sisters fell to his charms, or lusted for his knowledge, and a brother also. Shurilgar nurtured a plot to kill the king and raise Carnhaina as queen of Cardoroth, but when Carnhaina discovered it she repented. She disavowed him, and warned the king. But Shurilgar, seeing his plans wither before him, was not willing to pluck dry fruit from the vine of his ambition. He came for the king, gathering with him Ginhaina and the tainted brother, Felhain. With them were other traitors."

Gil's horse slipped on the wet grass, then righted itself. Gil barely paid any attention, he was transfixed by the story, for this was a version of it that he had not heard before.

"A mighty battle was fought," Brand continued. "There was sorcery and the flashing of swords. Blood flowed in the palace, even in the king's own room where he and the queen were brought to bay. Yet Carnhaina and her loyal brothers were there. If not for her, then they would have perished. Yet before it was all done, and Shurilgar defeated and fled, three of those brothers were killed."

Brand pulled his cloak tightly about him. A chill wind rose now with the rain, and it cut through them all. But Brand showed no sign of discomfort. He kept speaking.

"There in that room was first uttered the Durlin creed:

Tum del conar – El dar tum!
Death or infamy – I choose death!

What is not known is this. The motto was inspired by the fact that it was the betraying brother who had given him his death wound. That brother was said to have answered his father's condemnation with these words.

Tum del conar – El dar conar!
Death or infamy – I choose infamy!

Down through time the first brother's courage, loyalty and words are remembered. Of the traitor, only the Durlin keep record of what was spoken in their secret histories. And now you know it. We keep it alive to honor the first, to respect that each man and woman makes their own choices, and sometimes live and die by them. That first brother was a hero. He was a great man, and every day the Durlin strive to honor his memory and live up to his example."

Brand gestured at the sword belted at Elrika's side. "That blade was his. It hung on the wall in the room where all this happened so long ago. His hands touched it. He fought his enemies with it. And I think he would be proud to know that it is now yours. For you are like him: courageous and loyal."

Brand ceased speaking. The wind whipped about them and the rain angled sideways. No one said anything else.

Gil looked at Elrika. He could see her working through what Brand had said. He could almost hear her own doubt, wondering if she were worthy of the sword and Brand's comments. He knew she was, but did she?

Brand guessed what she was thinking also. He reached out, placing a hand on her shoulder.

"We all doubt our worth at times. But we do what we must anyway."

Suddenly the regent shuddered, and a strange look passed over his face while his eyes grew distant. Then he was himself again.

Brand looked back and forth between her and Gil. "You two, stay close to each other."

Elrika seemed confused, but Gil nodded. Brand had seen a vision, perhaps some glimpse of the future. Use of the magic tended to bring such a thing to the surface, but he knew Brand would not speak of it. Not yet anyway. Perhaps later.

The White Lady had been listening intently, and she spoke, directing her words at Elrika.

"Do not fear. You will acquit yourself well. This Brand knows, as do I." She looked then at Gil. "So will you, even if you do not like what you must do. Sometimes there are no right choices, but we do what we must anyway."

The White Lady's pale face was wetted by rain, but Gil thought he saw tears in her eyes too. But he could not be sure. Whatever vision it was of the future that Brand had just seen, she knew already, had long known it.

12. The Game is Up

Tainrik eased forward into the hollow. Immediately, the smell of smoke grew stronger. He could not see anything yet, but the fire must be close. Once again, he tried to reason how many people could be here, but there was no answer to that. The only way he could find out was to get closer.

This much was true though. He must assume it likely that it was a small group of men, and that there would be a lookout guarding their camp. Given this, and that the men and the lookout would be stationary while he must move, the advantage was with them.

Where, exactly, would they camp? If it were him, he would choose a place at the very bottom of the hollow. That would best hide light from the fire. And he would build the fire close to the base of a tree so that its canopy dispersed the smoke instead of allowing it to rise in a plume. He would also want his back to the steepest bit of the gully. This would prevent someone attacking from that side. At least, he would do it this way, and from what he could tell so far these men had skill.

One achingly slow step after another, taking his time to be completely noiseless, he moved deeper into the gully. Smoke was strong in the air now, and he must be close to the camp, very close, but still he saw nothing save for the dim outline of shrubby trees and a patchy sky of muted stars and scudding cloud through the foliage.

He paused. It was time to wait. Standing there, silent as the trees about him, like another trunk in the shadows, he strained all his senses for some sign of what he was getting into. But he detected nothing more than the smoke.

He had a choice now. Go ahead and try to avoid stumbling into the camp, or try for a different view on things. The trees allowed for that. He eased to the closest one, slipped his bow over his shoulder and carefully climbed it.

He did not intend to climb high. Just a few feet would give him a better view. But it was risky. He was much more likely to make noise and would be more visible. But he did it anyway. It was riskier to walk into the middle of the camp by accident and step on a sleeping man.

At last! He found what he had been seeking. A little further down the gully was a flicker of firelight. It was just the sort of place that he had expected, set up with a steep slope behind it and beneath a tree.

He studied the camp carefully. It was some fifty feet away, and there were men near the fire. He watched them closely, counting four. Two seemed to be sleeping, laying down and still, the others were seated on a fallen log and talking quietly.

There was no lookout. Or, if there were, Tainrik could not see him. Were they spies though? He could see no indication one way or the other. There were no visible axes, so they may not be foresters. But they could be hunters. Or the axes may be lying on the ground or embedded in blocks of wood elsewhere. There was no way to tell, especially without seeing the men and the camp properly.

It was obvious what had to be done, but he did not like it. Still, he forced himself to make the decision he knew he must. He lowered himself down from the tree, thankful that he made no noise, and then he edged closer to the camp.

Silently, he drew one of his knives. If things went wrong he would have a better chance to use it than anything else. The bow would be slow at close quarters.

He held the blade low before him, the steel of it darkened by a special tint during the forging process so that it did not glint in the night. Bit by bit, step by step, he drew closer. For all that he moved with great slowness, his heart raced in his chest as though he were sprinting.

Pausing, he took some long and slow breaths to calm himself. He could now hear the men talking. They were speaking loudly, or more likely he had crept closer than he thought.

"The rain will come soon," one man said. His accent was of Cardoroth.

"It'll slow the army," the second answered.

"Good."

"It'll help us though," the second man said.

"I still hate it. I'd rather be at home than stuck out here."

Tainrik listened. Both men were from Cardoroth, and their talk soon turned to the city. In particular, they spoke of an inn where the hearth-fire was always lit, the room warm and where the mead was sweet and smooth. Better there than here they thought, but they would return there when they could.

The speakers were silent for a while. One of the sleeping men began to snore, then ceased after a few moments. The two men awake carried on their conversation.

"What do you think Hvargil will do?" the first man asked.

"Kill Brand and the prince, for sure. He can do damage to the army, but he doesn't have enough men to keep it up for long. And why bother anyway? He'll want that army for himself."

"Do you think he has a chance?"

"With the regent and the prince out of the way, he does. He's in tight with many of the nobles. And he'll be the last of the true royal line then. Besides, if he kills them, he's done that black sorceress a favor. She may just leave us alone with *him* in charge. The nobles will know that, and those that don't he'll soon tell. It's quite a bargaining point."

Silence filled the gulley again, and Tainrik thought hard. The rumors were true, and these hills were where Hvargil and his outlaws hid. Given that these four men were hanging back behind the army, it seemed likely that another of their number had already left to take word to Hvargil. The old king's brother will know that Cardoroth's army was on the march.

What to do about it all was the problem. Tainrik had learned what he needed most to know, and his first priority was to give warning to Brand of a probable ambush and assassination attempt. The men in this camp were not so important now. And there were too many for him kill anyway. He must leave, and then come back with a larger group of scouts.

He took a step back, testing the ground lightly with his toes before putting his weight down. At just that moment he heard a whisper of movement behind him. He dropped to the ground, but he was too late. A thrown knife struck his left shoulder and pain flared. There was a lookout after all!

The game was up now. He had been discovered, and silence and stealth were useless. He rolled, sprang to his feet and ran.

It was hard to see, and he feared a thousand obstacles that he could trip over or run into, but speed counted now or he was dead. At the last moment he saw a fallen log and leaped it. He dodged left around a tree trunk and saw a shadow loom up to his right. The lookout!

He flung his dagger at the dark figure, and heard a grunt and saw the man go down. But he did not think he had killed him. It was just a wound and the man had dropped for cover as much as anything else.

Tainrik sprinted on. He heard shouts behind him, and crashing noises through the trees and underbrush. All the men were up, and they were coming after him.

13. A Game of Dice and Truth

The rain fell without relent. But the army was higher up in the hills now, and had reached the plateau. It continued on until late afternoon, for stopping was no better than proceeding.

All about them the forest grew thickly, but there were large patches of grassland too. Wild cattle, long-horned and wary, watched them from a distance. There were herds of horses too, likely escaped from Cardoroth through the long years. These wheeled away and filtered into the trees when the army came in sight.

The generals called a halt. This time, Brand was not unhappy. The army had traveled well, especially in the conditions, and where they had come to was a good place to camp. Because of the open space, the tail of the army eventually caught up and they were not spread out and vulnerable.

It did not take long to establish a camp, and it was formed in a great square. This offered good defense in all directions, and the sentries and scouts would provide warning of any attack. Water was to hand, and a clear view of the surrounding countryside.

Gil rubbed his horse down. It was common practice to dig a trench around the camp and throw up an earth wall when in hostile country. This was not being done, but he supposed there was no real reason to consider this hostile territory. Then again, he knew that was an assumption. They had not yet received any word from scouts that Ginsar's army had marched, but such a message may not reach them much before Ginsar. Or not at all if the enemy scouts had found and killed Cardoroth's.

By the time he had finished with his horse the camp was more or less established, and where once was green grass was now a sea of mud, people and tents.

He walked back with Brand and Elrika to where their own, and quite large tent was now set up.

"I'm worried, Gil," the regent said. "Tainrik is reliable, and I still have not heard from him."

"I know. But he would have to cover much more ground than the army did, and perhaps you'll see him tonight. He must sleep as well, at some point."

Brand retrieved a dry cloak and suggested Gil and Elrika do the same. Then they went out into the rain again. There was no sign of the generals. They had gone into their even larger tent, and there, likely, they would stay. But Gil had an idea that neither he nor Elrika would be under cover for a long time yet.

He was not surprised when Brand led the way back into the army again. They moved through the ranks, talking with men here and there, sharing a cup of water or a bite of food as they spoke. As always, Brand was just one of the soldiers, and though they knew who he was, they treated him as such, offering heartfelt opinions or boisterous jokes in turn.

Brand, for his part, was more at ease than ever. Gil studied him, and after a while began to adopt the same easygoing attitude. Elrika seemed to enjoy this, for she too was like Brand. But the soldiers loved teasing Gil good naturedly about his fine clothes and how wet and muddy they now were. He shrugged those comments off with a smile and a joke at their own expense. This they seemed to love above all, and he left many a tent of laughing soldiers behind him.

Yet there was something more serious going on here. Brand did this because it was in his nature to do it, but it was also a way of staying in touch with the men and assessing their morale. Even, perhaps, lifting it. This was a lesson the generals should learn, instead of staying dry and aloof in their tents.

They moved on, from tent to tent, and here and there ate of the cold rations the soldiers were given. There were no fires tonight, and it was a cheerless dinner mostly of hard-dried biscuits, but food was food and the men made their own cheer.

Gil noticed that no matter Elrika's casual attitude, she was always close by his side and alert. Brand noticed it too, and though he said nothing he seemed pleased. The story of the sword she carried had made a strong impression on her.

A man stopped Brand just as they were about to leave a tent. "Why are we here and not in Cardoroth?" he asked. It was an honest question, posed without malice, and Brand gave an honest answer.

"If the generals had their way, we *would* be in Cardoroth. And we'd be warm and snug too. But when Ginsar comes, she will bring sorcery with her. Powerful sorcery that would destroy us. We go now to meet her, to claim victory before the power she summons is too much. We go to surprise her."

"Will we win?" another soldier asked.

"I'll not lie," Brand answered. "I don't truly know. But I'll try my hardest, and I know too that every man in this camp will do the same. For what it's worth, I think that will be enough."

"It's good enough for us," the first man said. "We don't know magic and sorcery, but we trust you. You'll do your bit, and we'll do ours."

"I know it," Brand said.

They left the tent and moved on. Several times men asked the same question, and Brand gave the same honest answer. After a while, Gil realized it was not the question that counted. It was that the men felt they could ask it and that Brand gave them a truthful answer that counted.

After a few hours, they retuned back to their own section of the camp.

"Come with me for a few more moments," Brand said. "I want to speak with the generals."

They came to the generals' tent, and the guards there announced their names and guided them inside. All three of the generals were accommodated here, for it was a very large tent. There were inner partitions, rugs on the floor and a long table that ran down the center of the room. Upon it were the remains of several meals and three wrought-iron braziers, giving off warmth and light.

The generals lounged around the table, sipping wine and playing dice. Several piles of gold coins lay on the table.

"Please," Garling said. "Have a seat."

"We won't be staying long," Brand said. "It's late already."

Gil noticed that Brand remained standing, so he did not move either.

"Has there been any word of significance from the scouts?"

"Nothing of note," Garling answered.

"They have all returned? No one is missing?"

"Indeed not. All is well, though we're still waiting on reports from those scouts monitoring Ginsar's army. There's no word on her movements yet."

"I see," Brand said. "That's all I wished to know. Have a good evening gentlemen."

He left the tent, his expression neutral but the signs of anxiety were there for Gil to read. He did not think the generals knew him well enough to detect them.

They went to their own tent, smaller and less luxurious than that of the generals but still large. The Durlin opened the flap for them, and Brand said goodnight and immediately went to his own partitioned area. There were other partitioned rooms for Taingern and Shorty, but no sign of them.

Elrika looked at Gil with wide eyes. "Brand's trying to hide it, but he's very worried about Tainrik."

Gil nodded. He began to fear that something very bad had happened.

14. A Hunted Man

Tainrik continued to run. But he was no great sprinter, and he feared his pursuers would catch him. Nor would they have any trouble locating him in the dark because the sound of his flight as he crashed through the undergrowth could not be missed.

This could not go on and end well, so he made a swift decision. Even though his instinct was to try to run away, he paused abruptly and crouched down behind a large tree trunk.

The trunk was at his back and a large fern ahead. Between them both, the night-shadows were deep, and there was a fair chance he would not be seen. Stealth must serve him once more.

He sheathed the knife and nocked an arrow to his bow. Then he waited, trying to breathe as softly as he could. If all went well, they would run past and then he could slip away in the opposite direction.

The crashing noise of his pursuers came close. They were all around him in the dark. Then one of them yelled and Tainrik felt cold seep into his bones.

"He's stopped! Stand still and look!"

Tainrik felt a sense of dread threaten to overwhelm him. He forced himself to breathe smoothly though, and to remain perfectly still. The place of concealment that he had chosen was good, and he would not be spotted easily.

Silence fell. He heard nothing of the men, for evidently they dared not move just as he could not. To move was to chance revealing oneself, and that might mean sudden death.

He began to wonder how skilled these men were. The one who flung the dagger at him was good, for he had approached with silence and crept close. Unless he had been there all along, watching and waiting for his best chance to throw.

The wound to the shoulder that the man had given him began to throb. It had been a glancing strike of the blade only, but it had cut deep and he felt the blood from it trickle down his arm and begin to dry and cake. He wanted to check it to see just how bad it was, but he did not dare to move.

The temptation came upon him to run again, for natural instincts were hard to suppress. But it would be foolish. The men were closer to him now than before and would catch him swiftly, perhaps even kill him before he took more than a few steps. No, he must keep playing the game he had chosen.

Patience would serve him here. If they moved first, they would reveal themselves. Then he must throw a knife or fire an arrow. The first allowed him multiple opportunities for it was swift and he had the knives. The second more likely to kill, but he would likely only have one chance. He was ready with bow and arrow though, and that was perhaps the best. If he could be sure of killing one of the enemy, his odds against the others would improve. Somewhat.

A new thought came to him, and he did not like it. They may wait patiently for the dawn, still hours away, and let light reveal him.

He waited, his thoughts drifting and he lost track of time. He eased back slightly until he rested against the tree trunk behind him. He could not maintain a crouch forever. But it was not safe to stand, and nor could he sit because then he would be slow to move when movement was necessary.

His thoughts ceased to drift and he became suddenly alert. He was not sure what had changed, but his instincts were warning him of something. His gaze searched the shadows, and he concentrated on using his peripheral vision. In the dark, that would reveal something better than a direct line of sight.

There! A man, crawling on the ground. At least he thought so. But then there was nothing. Yet in a minute or so in the same place the movement began again and he was sure. His stalker was moving only a few feet at a time. And he was good for he made no noise.

At the current angle the man was going, he would move past him. But if Tainrik could see him, soon the man would spot him also.

Tainrik tested the fit of the arrow that he had notched to the string. Satisfied, he drew slowly, with as little movement as he could manage, and prepared to shoot. He let out his breath ever so slowly and at the end released the string.

The arrow flew. Its sudden flight hissed through the air and the crawling man half jumped up and then fell. He did not move again.

What to do now? Tainrik's mind raced. He may well have given his position away. Even as he remained where he was, the other men could be moving in on him. Yet to move was to highlight himself for attack. He remained still, moving only enough to slip another arrow from the quiver and nock it.

Tainrik's hands trembled. He had been trained for this, but the reality was different from the teaching. Every choice he made was one of life or death. And the throbbing in his shoulder made it hard to think clearly.

But he waited, knowing it was the right move, and he took some satisfaction from the fact that if he were to be killed tonight he had taken at least one of the enemy with him.

It grew darker. The cloud cover was building, and the stars were blotted out. There! It was a noise to his left and he flicked his gaze in that direction. He rose ever so slightly, drawing back on the string once more. But there was nothing to be seen.

What had he heard then? The answer was swift in coming. It was a thrown rock and he had exposed himself. In one smooth motion he dived and rolled. Even as he came to his feet again he felt an arrow slam into his left arm and then glance away into the night.

It did not stop him. Better the arm than the body it would have been if he had not disrupted his enemy's aim. With a burst of speed he sprinted again, leaping over the corpse of the slain man and crashing through the shrubbery.

Another arrow flew at him, whistling away well wide of his position. Yet one more thudded into a tree close to his head. But he was up and away and already lost to sight. They must chase him again or fire blindly into the dark.

He sped on, snaking between trunks. The ground began to rise, and this was not good. He would be more exposed above his enemies. He changed direction, veering abruptly to the left and following a downward slope.

Noise of pursuit gathered behind him. A small stream loomed ahead and at the last moment he leaped it. Straightaway he veered right, hoping to somehow evade those who hunted him. His maneuver was not successful. Arrows hissed through the dark, unseen but deadly. He had dodged in the wrong direction and brought himself back into view.

He could not turn left, for that would be predictable. Instead, he veered further right and up the slope again. More arrows hissed, but these went wider of him.

His chest heaved now for breath, and the slope did not help. But swifter than he had anticipated he found himself at the top of the gulley again. He raced away with a burst of speed, but his legs were giving out.

Ahead, the forest grew thicker. At least, so he thought because the shadows were even deeper. This offered greater chance of concealment, and he did not change direction.

The forest swiftly grew near-impenetrable, but he pushed on for another fifty or so paces, hearing his enemies enter the same area of thicker growth somewhere behind him.

It was time to rely on his skills as a tracker and woodsmen again, rather than try to run. Ahead, he saw the dim outline of a branch about head high and an idea occurred to him.

With trembling hands he tore off his cloak and looped the top portion over the trunk so that the remainder draped down near the trunk, and then he ducked and crawled a dozen feet away, coming up behind a fallen log. He waited, trying to breathe quietly.

In moments, his pursuers were close, but they slowed and then stopped too as they failed to hear him anymore. Once again, a game of patience had begun. This time there was one less of them, but they still outnumbered him.

There was no noise. Once more the forest was silent, yet the dark carried a feel of unmistakable malice. Danger and death hid in every shadow. But Tainrik gritted his teeth, vowing silently that he was as dangerous as anything in the woods tonight. Perhaps the *most* dangerous thing there.

Time passed. His hunters were wary of him now, and well they should be. But they had not given up. That, he knew. They would wait and watch, and perhaps try to move silently, searching for him as they had before.

Blood dribbled down his left arm. The arrow wound hurt less than the shoulder one, but was more of a problem. His arm felt weak and useless now. But he would not bleed to death from it.

He checked his bow. As he feared, somewhere when he rolled or ran through the trees the string had caught and been damaged. He felt loose strands and severe fraying. Dare he risk using it again? If it gave out on him when loosing an arrow he would be at great risk. He had a spare string in his pocket, but he did not think it wise to unstring the bow and string it again. That would be too much movement.

Softly, he placed the bow on the ground and drew one of his throwing knives. And waited once more.

15. More Terrible than You Know

Gil talked softly with Elrika in the tent, and the White Lady joined them. "You all seem anxious," she said.

Briefly, Gil explained to her about Tainrik. She closed her eyes momentarily, as if in deep thought.

"I wish I could help, but I cannot. Many things I can see, but not all. I seek him out, but find only blackness."

"He'll return," Gil said. "Something has happened, but he's the sort of man who overcomes any obstacle."

The White Lady opened her eyes. "But the absence of this scout isn't your only concern, is it?"

Elrika hesitated, then spoke. "It's not my place to say it, but I'm worried about Brand. He does not show it, but I sense that he feels enormous responsibility."

Gil nodded. "I feel it too. The generals wanted to stay behind the Cardurleth. Coming out to face Ginsar was his idea. If it fails, he will bear the blame."

"The answer to that is simple," the White Lady told them. "We must not fail. Though until we succeed, Brand will be under great strain. But he, like this Tainrik you know, is a man who overcomes obstacles."

"Do you really think we can win?" Elrika asked.

The White Lady turned to her, and her gentle face was determined. "We *must*. And this is in our favor. Brand is a canny man. He has endured and survived dangers that would have destroyed most people. More than that, he has luck. He is a man who makes his own luck by courage and skill and the sharpness of his wit, yet fate also smiles upon him. Nor is he alone. We will each play our part to help him. So, yes, we can win. But it will not be easy."

"The Horsemen will be the worst of it, won't they?" Gil asked.

"They are more terrible than you know," the White Lady answered. "Worse, the spell that binds them weakens. Ginsar can feel it. Should the worst happen, they will possess her. Then they will control their bridge into this world and using Ginsar, they can summon more of their kind."

"And this world," Gil said, "whence you and the Horsemen come, what is it like?"

The White Lady grew quiet, and Gil did not think she would answer. But eventually her reply came, though it was softly spoken.

"Our worlds should not be in contact. It is best not to speak of it. If all goes well, then the gateway will be closed and things shall return to how they should be."

"And what of you?"

She gazed at him, her eyes sad but lit with determination. You will see, and you will understand when the time is right."

She excused herself then, going to that portion of the tent partitioned off for her.

Elrika watched her go, then spoke quietly. "I like her, but she's hiding something. Something big."

Gil agreed, and it troubled him. But what it was they would not discover this night. He and Elrika said goodnight and moved into their own rooms within the tent.

By himself, Gil became thoughtful. But lying down on the thick rug that was his bed, he went to sleep swiftly, lulled by the constant patter of rain on the canvas roof.

He slept well, waking before dawn the next morning and feeling refreshed. There was movement within the main room of the tent, and he dressed and went outside.

Brand was there, moving slowly through some exercises. They were of a kind that Gil had not yet learned and his interest was piqued.

The regent moved slowly, as though fully relaxed, and yet Gil saw the slight tremble of his hands that indicated, despite the smooth stretching and grace of each movement, that muscular force was being used.

He saw that the White Lady and Elrika were already there, watching also. But of Shorty and Taingern there was no sign.

Brand breathed out softly and finished.

"That was beautiful," Elrika said. "Would you teach me?"

"Of course," Brand said. "But we have little time before the march begins. So I shall teach you some, and then if you are interested we will make time daily hereafter."

Elrika stood up and Gil joined her. He too wanted to learn the movements.

"Each exercise has a name," Brand said. "But don't be fooled by their slowness. There is within them a kernel of the warrior's art, and though the movements are for health, they will sharpen your combat skills too."

Brand stilled himself, standing with his feet shoulder width apart. "This first exercise is called *Scoop the Stream and Press the Stars.*"

He bent down smoothly as though cupping water in his palm and then straightening to drink. But he did not stop. Instead, he pushed upward toward the sky.

"It's important," he said, "to link the motion of your body with your breathing. Breathe in as though you were scooping air into your lungs and breathe out as you press upward."

They did that a few times. "Now," Brand continued, "do the same thing, but gently flex your muscles as you move. Do not be stiff though."

"How much tension should there be?" Elrika asked.

"Stop just when your arms begin to tremble," Brand said. "The movements stretch and limber the body, but at the same time they build muscle."

They practiced for a little while and then a soldier brought in some food. They sat down around the table and ate, glad to do so even if it was only the same army biscuits that they had eaten last night.

The White Lady noticed the ring on Brand's finger that he always wore, and Brand saw her looking.

"It's an ancient piece of jewelry," he said. "The spirit of Carnhaina gave it to me."

"You earned it," she said. "That much I know, but may I look at the ring closely?"

Brand removed it and handed it to her. She held it up and studied it carefully, turning it to and fro in the pale light of the lamps that lit the tent.

"It is ancient indeed," she said. "But there is power in it too."

"Magic?" Brand said. "I've never sensed it."

"Yet it is there, though buried deep and of an unusual sort. In time it may reveal itself to you." She turned it again, pausing. "There is a word inscribed inside the band. *Carngin*."

"Ah, I had forgotten that was there. Of old, the royal family of Cardoroth had two names. One was for private use among friends and family, while the other was for public use. Carnhaina's real name was apparently Carngin."

The white Lady handed the ring back and Brand slipped it onto his finger again.

"It is a marvelous piece of craftsmanship," she said. "But the magic in it is greater still. One day you will use it for its purpose, I am sure."

Gil was surprised. "I've never sensed any magic within it either," he said.

The White Lady turned to him, her eyes intense. "Sometimes the best hidden remains in plain sight."

He thought she was trying to tell him something, but had no time to consider it. At that moment the tent-flap was pulled open and a Durlin entered.

"The generals want to see you," he said to the regent.

16. A True Warrior

Tainrik continued to wait, but it was becoming harder. The wounds in his arm and shoulder were throbbing, and the muscles all over his body had stiffened.

But then he heard a noise, and all his aches and pains were forgotten. He looked and listened for what seemed a long while, but there was nothing else. Yet someone was close, and had moved. That he had begun to do so meant it likely that he would continue.

Waiting with all the patience that Tainrik had developed through long years of training, he calmed himself as best he could and remained motionless.

Eventually, his patience was rewarded. There was a scuffling sound close by, and the hand that gripped his knife became slick with sweat.

Then he saw what he had been waiting for, hoping for. A little more than a dozen feet away a man slowly rose and drew a bow. With a twang he unleashed the arrow and it whistled though the air, striking the cloak.

Tainrik was already moving. The man was further away than he hoped, but with a swift motion he flung his throwing dagger. It arced and spun through the air.

The man was turning, realizing he had been tricked. But he was too slow. The flashing blade thudded deep into his belly.

The man grunted with pain. But he made to pull a second arrow from his quiver. Tainrik ran at him, drawing another knife. There was no time for the man to loose the arrow he had retrieved. Tainrik thrust his blade forward, but even as he did the man smashed the bow against his face.

Pain erupted in Tainrik's head, but he felt his blade drive deep in the other man's groin. His enemy screamed, then reeled away and fell to the ground. He was dead, or soon would be when he finished gushing blood.

Tainrik darted forward, grabbed his cloak and sprinted again. He had hoped to kill the man and stay hidden where he was, but luck had not favored him. The man had been too far away to risk a killing throw to his neck. Instead he had been forced to throw for the body, which had not been an instant kill.

Blood ran down his face, and the fresh injury hurt with a sharp pain. Skin was torn, but no bones broken. Yet his legs were unsteady and he felt a wave of nausea. He leaped a log and nearly fell, for dizziness swept over him too.

Stumbling, he tried to right himself but staggered to the side. It saved his life. An arrow hissed past him and he felt the wind of it.

Fear drove him on, and despite dizziness he staggered ahead. But the dizziness soon receded even if the nausea did not.

Another arrow whined nearby, slamming into a tree trunk. He veered left, fell, came to his feet with a roll and sped on.

The ground changed swiftly, and he nearly fell again but adjusted quickly. He was heading downhill once more. He slowed a little, but another arrow flashed past him and he put on a burst of speed.

It was a mistake. He lost his footing on the slope and crashed into the ground, tumbling and spinning through ferns and underbrush. He had tried to break his fall with his arms, but his left had given way beneath him and sent a jab of pain like fire through the whole limb.

He staggered up, wet and muddy, somewhere near the bottom of the gulley. It must have been the same one that he had left earlier, but he was becoming disorientated.

Moving ahead he plunged into water without seeing it. He fell again, righted himself and stumbled ahead.

Water soaked his clothing. His wounds stung and now there was mud in them. If his enemies did not kill him, blood loss or infection might. He pushed ahead anyway, hearing his hunters come down the slope somewhere behind him.

Coming to the bank at the other side of the gulley he ran uphill. An arrow sped through the air, but it was well away from him and he guessed that his opponents were becoming frustrated and loosing arrows at him too quickly to aim properly.

He reached the crest and dared to turn for a look. He cursed his luck, for he saw a man climbing up after him but he had no bow to shoot with, and even if he had not left it at his last hiding place the string may have broken.

But he chanced another knife throw even at such a distance, and sent a blade flashing through the air. The man screamed and fell back. Tainrik turned and ran on wondering if perhaps his luck was not all bad.

He went a little ahead but soon the landscape changed. It was much more open, becoming a little clearing, and he decided to stop. It was not a good place to hide, but his strength was nearly gone. Better to fight now before it all drained away, than to prolong things.

He slipped behind a tree and drew his sword. It was not a place of good concealment, but it was dark and would have to do. The men behind him outnumbered him two to one, but he had brought the odds down greatly, if still not in his favor.

Quickly he discarded his quiver. It would only hinder him now. But no sooner had he placed it on the ground than he sensed his hunters close by.

They knew he was wounded and tired now. That much they would have been able to tell by the way he moved, but they may also have seen blood where he had hidden. There was certainly enough of it left behind.

He swayed slightly, feeling blackness descending over his mind, but he fought it and stayed on his feet. He would not die by having his throat cut as he lay unconscious on the ground. If he were to live and bring word back to Brand he must force a swordfight, and then somehow win it against two men. He was not even a great swordsman, but he was skilled, and he doubted his opponents were as good.

He saw them approach, but they had not yet seen him. They stayed together now, sure that they were near to hunting him down and determined not to be picked off one by one as their companions had.

Tainrik smiled grimly in the dark. One of the men moved forward, his hand held up and pressed against his shoulder. He was the lookout who had been wounded when the chase began.

So far so good. That improved the odds a little, but both men had drawn their swords just as he had done. They *knew* he was close.

Slowly, Tainrik drew his last knife. He was right handed, but his sword was in that hand. He used his left, and though not as good with that arm he had practiced hard and gained skill with it.

The two men saw him. He reacted instantly, flinging the knife at the unwounded man. Better to face the wounded one in a swordfight.

The man dodged to the side, but not quick enough. The blade tore at his throat and a spray of blood erupted. Arterial blood.

Tainrik stepped from the shadows, sword high. The enemy he had struck stumbled away, pressing his hands to his throat, but the wounded man leapt at him, trying to ensure nothing could be flung at him.

With a crash of steel against steel Tainrik met him. Out in the open, the first pale glimmer of dawn showed him his enemy. A large man, red-haired and bearded, as skilled with a blade as he was at woodcraft.

The first touch of their blades revealed to Tainrik that they were closely matched. They were also both wounded, yet the other man far less so. But the injury was to his enemy's sword arm, and that was an advantage.

They circled, but the red-haired man seemed angry and he charged in swiftly with an overhead strike.

Tainrik almost fell for it. He began to raise his own blade to block the blow but then stepped to the side. He was just in time. For all his enemy's size he was quick. Even as he swung his sword his other hand flicked out a knife.

The blade sailed away harmlessly through the air. Tainrik, seeing an opportunity, drove forward himself. He launched a vicious flurry of blows, and his enemy retreated but blocked and deflected the attack until Tainrik began to slow. Then he retaliated with his own attack.

The big man came at him, sword flashing and eyes cold with the promise of death. Tainrik retreated now, trying to conserve his strength and using his footwork to keep out of reach and minimize the effort he put into blocking.

The attack petered out and the two men circled each other warily now. Both were short of breath. Both were in pain from their wounds. Both were uncertain of the outcome of this fight.

But the big man regained his breath more quickly. His blade sliced the air, flicking unexpectedly toward Tainrik's neck. Tainrik jumped back, but only just in time. Then a series of other blows came at him, and he suffered glancing slashes to his right shoulder and left flank.

Tainrik did his best to defend. He was weary now, more than he had ever been in his life, and he knew that was blood loss as well as tiredness. Nor had the dizziness completely left him. The sense of blackness engulfing him was never far away, and several times it threatened to send him to his knees. But he stayed upright, and he staved off the killing blows that came at him.

His red-bearded attacker circled once more, and for the first time he spoke.

"You're nearly done, dog. I think I'll cut you apart, piece by piece."

Tainrik grinned. This was good! The man was taunting him now, which meant that his continued survival had gotten under his opponent's skin and frustrated him. It also meant that he too was tired.

Now, if ever, was Tainrik's chance. This could not go on for much longer, and he wasted no effort on replying. Instead, he darted forward thrusting at the man's face.

His opponent backed away, which was what Tainrik had hoped for. He skip-stepped ahead once more and flicked his sword using little more than the power of his wrist. It was a swift move, and unexpected. Brand had shown it to him long ago, and now it worked.

His blade glanced across his enemy's neck while the man began to swing a mighty blow, thinking Tainrik fully extended. Instead he jerked and reeled away as he felt the blade.

Tainrik knew instantly that he had not delivered a killing blow, but the man had been cut and surprised.

Tainrik pressed forward, changing tactics now and striking at his enemy's sword arm.

His opponent rallied, fending off the blows but he did not see the left fist that cracked against his skull as Tainrik simultaneously struck at his wrist and punched.

Pain roared through Tainrik's injured arm, but his enemy had turned to the side exposing his flank and Tainrik lunged forward, sliding his blade between the man's ribs.

The red-bearded man jerked away and collapsed, nearly pulling Tainrik's sword clear. Red foam frothed at his lips and his expression was one of surprise as he died.

Tainrik stood still, watching him. It was all he could do to keep a grip on his sword without letting it fall and remain standing upright. But he had won, defeated all his opponents. He was just as surprised as the dead man at his feet.

He tried not to, but he turned and kneeled on the grass and vomited. A long while he retched, and he felt so weak that he feared he would not be able to stand. Eventually, cold and shivering in the dawn light, he staggered upright.

His sword still drawn, he moved over the man he had brought down with the thrown knife. Checking that his enemy was dead, he cleaned his sword blade on the man's cloak and sheathed it. Then he retrieved the knife from the grass nearby, cleaned it also, and sheathed it.

Feeling somewhat better, he retraced his flight and went down in the gulley. There was water there, and he needed to clean his wounds. He did not look forward to it, for it would hurt.

The body of the man he had killed down in the gully made him feel sick again. But he retrieved another of his knives. Of everything that had happened, killing this man had been the luckiest. It had been a long throw with little real chance of success. But somehow he had accomplished it, and it was the turning point. Had three men confronted him up in the clearing it would now be him lying on the ground, dead eyes staring up, unseeing.

He knelt down by the small stream. The water flowed, but it was not brisk. There was risk in using it to clean his wounds, but they were covered in mud anyway. They *had* to be cleaned, and the water was the only way of doing it.

He peeled off his tunic and bathed as best he could, being sure to remove the mud while at the same time not opening the wounds further. They bled again, which was no bad thing for the flow of blood would help remove more dirt. Then, retrieving thread and needle from an inner pocket he stitched the cut in his arm. It was hard to do, but he gritted his teeth and endured the pain.

His shoulder was harder, but he managed at length. It was his headwound that troubled him most though. He could not see it and did not know if it needed stitches. Regardless, it was a job beyond him, and all he could do was cut a strip of cloth from the dead man's tunic and wrap it around his head. It would have to be enough, at least until he could get back to camp.

The sun was well up now, its light penetrating even into the forested gulley. Tainrik felt sick, and desperately tired. All he wanted to do was lie down and sleep, but he must go on.

He shuffled forward, moving through the thick timber carefully. His bow could not be that far away, but he did not have the energy to search for it. He would risk travel without it, because it seemed unlikely that he would encounter further enemies.

What counted now would be catching up with the army, if he could. In his current state that was going to be very hard. He was well behind it and it would travel faster than he could. To reach it, he would have to travel by the open road. That was potentially dangerous. And he would also have to walk into the night long after the army had camped.

He came to a small clearing and shivered even in the sunlight. What lay ahead was going to test him. But Brand had to know what he had learned.

Moving into the trees and seeking the road he gritted his teeth and shuffled forward. He stumbled, righted himself and moved on again. He had hoped that walking would ease his sore muscles, but instead they began to cramp.

He pressed forward. He had just endured the longest night of his life. Now, the longest day lay ahead.

17. Dismissed

All three generals entered the tent, and Gil could tell that they were determined on some purpose.

"Welcome," Brand said. "Have a seat."

They pulled up chairs around the table, and there was much awkward shifting and scraping of chair legs against the canvas floor. Just as they were sitting, Taingern and Shorty also arrived in a rush. Gil could tell from their expressions that they were angry, but they said nothing.

As the Durlindraths took seats, Gil noticed that the generals looked displeased. He realized that they may have arranged to have someone lure Taingern and Shorty out of the tent in order to isolate Brand from his supporters.

"What news?" Brand asked.

"None," Garling answered. "And that is the problem."

"How so?"

"Our scouts report no sign of the enemy, and they have ventured far ahead of us."

"*How* far ahead?" Brand inquired.

"A day or so. They have found no indication of an army before us. Not even enemy scouts."

Brand shrugged. "That doesn't really mean much. We're still close to Cardoroth, and elugs aren't renowned for military strategy. They may not even use scouts."

"Preposterous!" Druigbar said. "All armies use scouts."

Brand's attitude seemed to cool, though he remained courteous. "Preposterous? I don't think so. In Cardoroth, you have had little dealings with elugs, and what dealings you have had has mostly been with those of the south rather than the north. And mostly you stay behind the Cardurleth. The Duthenor, on the other hand, have had more trouble. The northern elugs often come down out of the mountains and raid our lands. They have never used scouts, though I concede that does not mean they aren't now. In short, they may or may not. We don't know, and we shouldn't judge them by our standards of warfare."

"It does not matter either way," Garling said. "We don't think there are scouts because we don't think there's an elug army. It will have proceeded down the Halathrin road."

"Has there been any word yet from the scouts watching the area where Ginsar gathered the army near Auren Dennath?"

"No."

"Then we know nothing yet, either way."

"Those scouts may have been killed," Druigbar said.

"That's possible," Brand conceded. "But not likely. Nothing has changed to alter the strategy decided on in Cardoroth."

Garling slammed a hand down on the table. "Everything has changed!" he said. "The men are unhappy to leave their homes only weakly defended. They fear Ginsar will strike while we're out here. And it was just the wrong strategy to begin with."

The other generals nodded their agreement. Garling went on, but his tone softened. "It's party our fault. We are the military experts. We know what we're doing. We should not have been swayed by you, or the Durlindraths or the prince. But it's not too late to remedy that. We can fix this, while there's still time. We can turn around and go back."

"No," Brand said softly.

Garling looked like he was holding a great anger in check. "You can't just say no. That's unacceptable."

Brand seemed relaxed, but Gil knew his moods well. Just now he was a very dangerous man indeed.

"I'm the regent. I have the authority. I can say no, and I do say no. It's that simple."

"Are you an idiot, Brand!" Garling stormed. "You've never led a campaign before! You don't know what you're doing."

Brand sat back in his chair. "I appreciate your honesty. But, respectfully, you have never led a campaign either."

Garling clenched his fists. "I'm a general! I've lived and breathed war all my life. Cardoroth is like that. I've fought in many battles and I've—"

Brand interrupted him. "I'll say it again, respectfully. You have never led a campaign. Always, the old king was the strategist. He had full control of the army and you carried out his orders. Nor did you *fight* battles. You commanded men who fought battles. From a distance, those men tell me. Now, the decision has been made and we have no further information that would make us change it. The army will continue as planned."

Brand turned his gaze to look all three generals in the eye one at a time.

"Gentleman," he said. "In war, disunity is death. A divided leadership will do us more harm than the enemy could. We must be of one mind in all that we do. Can you commit to this?"

Garling shook his head. "No. If we are to be of one mind, you must change yours."

"I'm resolved on our current course of action," Brand told him.

Garling shrugged. "Then we are at an impasse. We will lead the army forward no further."

Brand leaned forward and spoke earnestly. "I ask you to reconsider, not for me but for the benefit of Cardoroth."

Gil studied the generals. They looked smug, as though they had maneuvered Brand into a position where he must give in. Gil wondered if they knew him at all.

"We three are of one mind. We will not lead the army further forward into folly."

Brand sat back in his chair. "A divided leadership is poison. I just cannot let that continue."

Garling seemed pleased with those words. "Then I'll give the order to turn around and return to Cardoroth."

"That's not what I meant," Brand told him.

"But you just said—"

"I said that we cannot continue with a divided leadership. Therefore, you are dismissed from your positions. You will play no further part in forming the strategy of the army. You are dismissed, gentlemen."

The generals seemed dumbfounded. "We were appointed by the king!" Garling said. "You can't dismiss us!"

"I've heard that phrase too often," Brand said. "I can dismiss you. I just have dismissed you. You, and many of the other nobles of Cardoroth, aren't quick learners."

Garling half stood in his chair and thrust a finger at Brand. "You'll cause a revolt," he said. "The men won't follow you forward. They'll return to Cardoroth with us!"

Brand seemed very calm. "Be careful. You're treading close to treason there."

Garling sat back down, uncertain. He seemed about to speak, but did not. Instead, Taingern did.

"You're wrong about the men," he said quietly. "There will be no revolt. They'll follow Brand's orders, and gladly. They love him, and they'll fight for him to the death. He is one of them, as you could never be, being nobles."

Gil knew that was true. He also better understood Brand's long walks through the camp. He had guessed the generals would try something like this and assessed the mood of the men to follow him instead of them.

The generals stood, and they seemed shocked and uncertain. This meeting had not turned out as they expected, and their bluff had been called. Only Garling managed to speak.

"You'll regret this, Brand. Time will prove us right."

"It may, Garling, but I don't think so. Anyway, this conversation is over. You may leave."

The generals stalked out. Brand waited until they were gone before he spoke.

"This isn't what I really wanted, at least not yet. But so be it. What it means though is that I must now rely more heavily on you all."

"Will you appoint new generals?" Gil asked.

"No. I'll now lead. You will take on a greater role, and I shall seek your opinions. That's as it should be. I'll also seek input from others in the army. I'll think on who they should be. For the moment, it's time to ride."

They left the tent, and soldiers swiftly began to dismantle it. The rain had cleared, and the army was prepared to march. Going to their horses, they found the generals mounting and ready to ride.

"If we're not wanted here," Garling said, "we'll take a guard and return to Cardoroth."

"I don't think so," Brand answered. "You'll stay where I can see you, and that will be riding close by me at all times."

He signaled Shorty over. "Keep an eye on them. They're to ride in our group and not leave it. Pass the word to the Durlin."

"As you wish," Shorty answered.

Brand turned to Taingern. "Bring all the colonels over to me. I'll speak to them before we set off."

Taingern left, and the generals fumed silently while the others saddled and mounted their horses.

Taingern returned soon after with the colonels, and Brand addressed them.

"Men, you will be aware that the generals and I do not agree on the strategy for this campaign. I have therefore relieved them of their command, and I now lead. You will take your orders directly from me now. Are there any questions?"

The men seemed uncertain, and one voiced his doubt. "Is this really going to help us win?"

Brand turned his gaze upon him, and smiled. "A good question, and a brave one. I am regent, but let no man here follow my orders without question. If you see something you think is wrong, say so. I will consider all your views. But once a decision is made, I expect you to follow it perfectly." He paused, looking around at the men, then glanced back at the man who had spoken. "To answer your question, yes, this will help us win. I could give you all the reasons why, but they would be mere words on the wind. Instead, I'll say this. I'm Brand. You know who I am and what I've done. Do you believe in me?"

Some of the men cheered. Others seemed in doubt. "That is enough for now. You will believe more as each day unfolds. Now, give the signal to the army and we'll march."

Garling fixed Brand with a knife-like stare. "I know, beyond doubt, that you'll regret this."

"It is possible," Brand answered calmly.

Ahead, the carnyx horn that signaled the commencement of marching was blown. The horn gave off an eerie sound, a sound out of the ancient past of the Camar people. Gil thought back to his ancestors who held the horns to be sacred. They had winded them in the tumult of battle and believed the sound scared their enemies. Well might it be so.

The army surged forward, some of the cavalry holding high the varied banners of Cardoroth, and Gil felt a surge of pride. These were his countrymen, marching to protect the nation, willing to risk their lives to do so. He would do no less. And he, like they, would follow Brand.

Onward the army marched and the morning passed. Gil had felt a strange thrill run through him at the sounding of the carnyx horn, as though it had stirred something ancient in his blood. That feeling had not left him. Rather, it intensified as the army went forward.

He rode ahead, less and less mindful of what was happening about him. The world receded and a vague dream-state took its place. He tried to shake it off, but could not. Unease rippled through his consciousness, but he seemed powerless to speak or signal Brand.

All at once the dream focused. Ginsar appeared before him, standing tall and regal as she always did. The sorceress was clad in white, and a silver crown was set upon her head. It gleamed and shone, contrasting against the midnight black of her long hair that streamed behind her in a breeze that did not touch Gil.

"Hail, Prince of Cardoroth," she greeted him.

"Hail, Queen of Sorcery," Gil answered. And though he spoke and knew that she heard him, he knew also that no one else could see her nor hear his voice.

"It is time that we talked again," she said. "And this time I shall say things that you most need to hear."

"Speak, then. I'm listening."

"Ah, that is because you must. This is no vision that you can banish as you did last time. I'm sure that frustrates you. But no matter. You will find it instructive to listen. Firstly, you should know that this magic is within your power. And so much more. But you do not delve into the

127

gift you have. That is a mistake, for few have your talent and it should not be thwarted. I could teach things to you, such things as would make your soul sing."

Gil tried with all his willpower to break free of the spell she had cast upon him, but he did not know how.

She smiled at him. "Does that not tempt you, young prince? To learn the Mysteries? To have power such as few could even dream of? To unravel the secrets of life and death? Look me in the eye and tell me that it is not so."

Gil gazed into her eyes. He could not help it. "Who does not wish these things?" he replied.

"Yes indeed. But they are denied to you. Instead you must one day be king. That is your duty." She paused and looked thoughtful. "But it need not be so. You could be king, yes. But you could also learn the Mysteries. You could be a sorcerer king."

Gil could not stop himself from looking at her, but some part of his mind rebelled. "I learn lòhrengai – I would never learn elùgai. Sorcery such as that is of the dark, and I reject it."

Ginsar considered him, and her expression was neither worried nor angry. "You are quite correct. I would teach you dark ways. But it is just a word. Elùgai is just a different expression of the same power. And in the end, it is just as much your heritage as the throne of Cardoroth."

Gil shook his head. He did not wish to argue with her, for he sensed that in this waking dream he could win no debate. But he knew it was important to resist.

"None of that is true," he said.

"Oh, it is true. And you know it. I see it in your eyes. Carnhaina herself was of the dark. She was very nearly an elùgroth, but she failed at the last. It need not be so with you…"

"It will *never* be so with me. I swear it."

128

She smiled at him again, and he sensed that in some way she had changed, but he was not sure in what manner.

"So sure? Wait and see. You will learn by the end that fate cannot be defied. It is in your blood, even as it is in mine."

Gil decided that this had gone on long enough. He could not break out of this dream, he did not have the strength to oppose her will. But was that the right approach? Brand had always taught him that strength against strength was not the way. Perhaps subtlety was needed instead.

He gathered the magic within him, felt it come alive with his thought. Then he sent out tendrils, felt them work their way around him, sensed the riders nearby, the army and the hills and forest. Then he hooked onto those feelings, the sensations of reality rather than dream, and let them pull him out of this waking dream, for great though Ginsar's power was, reality was stronger still.

Ginsar receded as the real world came back into focus. But he saw her throw back her head and laugh, and the whisper of her voice slipped into his ears before she disappeared.

"We will meet again, Prince of the Blood."

18. A Man out of Nightmare

On through the day the army proceeded, following the routine of march, rest and march again relentlessly. Of the waking dream that Gil had experienced and the words of Ginsar, he said nothing. Brand had enough to worry about as it was.

Finally, the end of the day came in a sunset of ruined clouds and rising mists on the high hills. The land seemed desolate, wild, born of ancient magic. It was not tame like Cardoroth, and Gil began to love it. For once, he envied Brand that he had traveled widely across Alithoras and seen the sun rise and set over unfamiliar views like this.

Here, the plateau of the hills seemed wide and open. But they were on its edge. Tomorrow, the road would plunge down through thick forests again, where the trees would crowd close and invoke a sense of unseen eyes watching. Thus it always seemed in the forest, but with Ginsar about and her army coming, those eyes may be real rather than imagined. And the army would be spread out and vulnerable once more.

The march ceased, ended by a wavering blast from the same carnyx horn that started it all those hours ago. Gil dismounted, taking off the saddle and rubbing down his roan, now a fixed part of his daily routine, and perhaps the best part of it.

By the time he finished, the posts for the picket lines had been prepared and attendants came with feed for the horses. The tent was also erected, and to this he returned with Brand and the others. There was little rest to be had though, at least not for Brand. Almost immediately scouts began to return, bringing with them news. The regent had instructed that they now reported directly to him. There was an endless stream of them, and though the reporting was time-consuming, Gil knew that intelligence of the land around an army and the movements of the enemy were critical to success.

The general indications were that signs of people in the forest had been discovered, though no one had actually been seen and it was unknown who, or how many, they were. There was a large village many miles to the west, though it had recently been abandoned. Whoever dwelt there would know the forest well though, and it was more than possible that they had learned of the marching of the army and dispersed.

Brand asked if it were possible that significant numbers of men could be nearby. The scouts assured him it was not, though there could easily be small groups that remained undetected.

Of the elug army, no evidence had been found, and there was still no word from the long-range scouts monitoring it.

Overall, Brand seemed relieved at the news the scouts brought, and the regent treated them well offering each one of them watered wine as they reported and words of thanks for their good work. Nevertheless, he gave instructions for the camp sentries to be doubled and extra precautions taken against possible attack by small groups.

When the influx of scouts ceased, the small group in the tent drank their own wine and enjoyed a simple but beautifully hot meal of stew and vegetables on stale bread.

Conversation was sparing, and there was a distant look in Brand's eyes. Gil wondered if he were analyzing the next steps of the army, or worrying about what had happened to Tainrik. Both, he concluded.

The evening passed quickly, and they soon retired to their separate compartments in the tent. However, Gil had barely gone to sleep when he heard a commotion outside and raised voices. Swiftly he pulled on his boots and belted his sword, and then he went out into the main room of the tent.

The others came out too. A single lamp still burned, giving off light to see by, and their faces were confused and worried. Was an attack on the camp underway?

Brand drew his sword and stepped forward toward the tent flap. He never reached it. The canvas was pulled open before him, and several figures entered. There were two Durlin, and they supported between them a man who staggered, a man covered in dried blood, his features twisted in pain and his body wracked by shivers and spasms.

"Tainrik!" Brand said hoarsely.

Gil recognized him now, though he was changed greatly. Not only had he been injured, with one eye swollen shut, but he was ill also with some fever that wracked his body and shone in his one open eye. His clothes were torn and ripped, and in some places the damaged cloth was caked by dried blood. These were not injuries, but battle wounds. He was a man walked out of nightmare, and how he had survived it Gil could not guess.

The regent sheathed his sword and retrieved a chair. Gently, the Durlin eased the man down upon it.

"What happened to you, my friend?" Brand asked, kneeling down and taking his hand.

Tainrik struggled to speak, but his voice was a dry croak.

Swiftly Gil fetched a goblet of water and made to hand it to the scout, but Tainrik's hands trembled too much to hold it properly. Gil helped him, steadying the goblet as they lifted it to his mouth to drink.

He gulped it down, and then looked like he might vomit it back up again. But he rallied and his shivering reduced.

"Trouble," he croaked. "Be careful, Brand."

Elrika had retrieved a blanket, which she wrapped around the man's shoulders, and Brand looked up at one of the Durlin. "Fetch a camp surgeon, and swiftly."

Tainrik shivered again. "I have news, friend."

"Wait," Brand said. "Drink some more water first."

Gil took the goblet and moved back to the table.

"Wine," Tainrik croaked, and Brand nodded his approval as Gil looked at him.

"Make it red wine, unwatered," the regent said.

Gil knew that red wine was supposed to help the body replace lost blood. If nothing else, it should make Tainrik feel better anyway. He filled the goblet and returned.

This time the scout sipped it, but he still needed help to hold the goblet steady.

"I have bad news, Brand," he said.

"It can wait. The surgeon will be here shortly, and when he's done then we can talk."

Tainrik shook his head. "Can't wait," he said softly.

Brand pulled up another chair and sat opposite him. "What news then?"

"We were followed … Found their camp … Heard them talk," Tainrik said breathlessly. Every word seemed to cost him to speak it, and Gil wondered at what the man must have endured to reach his present state, but how strong his willpower was to keep moving and reach the camp. Other men would have laid down and died somewhere back in the hills.

"Hvargil is here. In hills. He knows you're coming because a message was sent ahead." Tainrik coughed, his

133

whole body shuddering, but he went on. "His men think if you and Gil are killed, he is a chance of being king."

Brand looked thoughtful. "It's possible," he agreed. "More than possible. And you think there may be an ambush?"

Tainrik coughed again, unable to speak for a moment, but he nodded vigorously.

Brand reached out and placed a hand on his shoulder. "Then we'll be ready for it, thanks to you. You've done well, and I'll not forget it."

Gil considered how loyal Tainrik must have been to Brand. It had nearly killed him to bring this message. In fact, it might kill him yet. He knew he should not be surprised though. Brand had that effect on people. They knew he would do the same for them.

Taking the now empty goblet, Gil filled it with some more wine and returned. He helped Tainrik sip at it, but he looked at Brand.

"Hvargil is of the true line, as am I," he said. "Only the nobles like him. If you and I were both killed, I could see them turn to him."

"I think so," Brand agreed. "But Hvargil doesn't have the men to attack this army."

"No, but he could launch an ambush as you said, directed at you and me."

"Quite possibly. These large tents make us obvious targets at night." He turned to Taingern. "Warn the sentries that an attack is possible. And increase the guard."

Taingern left the tent and Brand turned back to Gil. "I would think though that an attack during day is more likely. There's a place ahead where an ambush could be set. The trail enters a gorge as it winds down the hills. If I were Hvargil, and had few men, that is where I'd snare my trap."

The White Lady bent over and whispered for a few moments in Brand's ear. A slow smile lit his face.

"That, lady, is exactly what we shall do." He beckoned Shorty over. "Alert the scouts," he ordered. "Tell them to avoid that gorge and the area surrounding it. The enemy know the terrain better than them, and they will be at risk of being killed for nothing." He paused, and then added angrily. "I suspect Hvargil is the reason we haven't heard any further word from the long-range scouts monitoring Ginsar's army. He'll come to regret that."

Gil was about to ask what plan Brand had, for certainly he and the White Lady had conceived one, but the surgeon arrived.

The healer was an older man, tall and strongly built. He looked more like a warrior than anything else, but his sharp eyes took Tainrik in at a glance. "You should be dead, son. But I've seen your type before. You'll live."

Gil looked at the scout, and was not so sure. But he hoped he survived, for he was the kind of man that Cardoroth needed, the kind of man that a king would draw to his side.

19. War!

The night was old, and mist rose like groping fingers from the river. Ginsar returned to the camp of her acolytes and wasted no time. More must yet be done before the darkness died and birthed the new day.

"Awake!" she cried, and the camp stirred to sudden life.

They came and gathered to her then, all her acolytes and the Lethrin and elug representatives. She paid the elug no heed, for his kind were of use to her only in large numbers. Not so the others.

She stood tall and regal, a figure of command. "The time has come. I have this night spoken with the dead and learned of the future. Time hastens. We will hasten with it, and rise over the land like a wave surging to victory. And when Cardoroth is destroyed, then why should all Alithoras not follow? And then, the very world! It is ours for the taking! Is this not what you have dreamed of?"

They answered her then with gleeful cries and cheers and clenched fists thrust into the air. All except the Lethrin who remained untouched by her words. She turned to him, and the others grew suddenly quiet.

She lowered her voice and spoke in little more than a whisper. "Why do you not cheer?"

The Lethrin gave an impassive shrug. "The words of the dead are always two-edged. Such is the lore among my people. The shade you spoke with would have uttered no words guaranteeing victory, and the import of what it did say would be couched in double meanings and dark riddles. Is it not so?"

Ginsar hissed, and the acolytes moved away from him, but the Lethrin stood his ground, unperturbed.

She smiled then, a sudden dazzle of genuine good humor. So few stood up to her. The Lethrin was *perfect* for her plans.

With a gesture she summoned an acolyte to stand close before her. "Olekgar, you are the youngest, and yet, the greatest among your brothers and sisters. Ever you grasp the subtleties of what I teach, and your mind nimbly moves to other possibilities building a tower of knowledge from the foundations that I provide. Therefore, you shall be rewarded."

Olekgar bowed, his fair hair spilling out from beneath the dark cowl. He straightened, and began to step back. No doubt he intuited what was coming next, but no matter.

Ginsar pointed at him and he stilled, held by invisible bonds.

"No, Mistress. Please. Not that."

She smiled sweetly at him but did not answer. Instead, she pointed at the Lethrin and cast a net of dark magic over him. The creature stiffened, not knowing what it meant but sensing danger. He tried to back away, but found himself stepping forward until he stood side by side with Olekgar.

"You shall be brothers," she said. "So different, and yet so much the same."

She pointed a finger at each, willing them to kneel before her, piling upon their shoulders a weight of irresistible sorcery.

Olekgar muttered some spell, trying to break free of the entrapment. She felt the force of it, the depth of his mind and the power that he summoned. She smothered it with her own dark power and his knees crumbled, sending him crashing to the ground, fear lighting his eyes.

The Lethrin did not move. There was a store of determination in his mind that surprised her. It would be easier to topple a mountain than him. But there were ways.

With a swift movement her hand flashed out, slapping the creature across the face. He staggered back, for she was far stronger than she looked. And in that moment of surprise she sent numbness into his legs and piled a redoubled weight of magic upon him so that he too, proud though he was, bent down before her and crashed to his knees. Rage burned in his eyes and his desire to reach out and kill her filled the air with palpable intent.

Ginsar drew her knife, a relic from ancient Cardoroth, and savored the moment the Lethrin saw it. His eyes locked onto hers and there was a rage within them terrible to behold, yet impotent. He could not move. She smiled. Oh, he was *perfect*.

The acolytes were silent and motionless, daring no movement that might draw attention to themselves. The mist on the river to her left stirred sluggishly. The higher ground to the right hulked like a mass of watching shadows in an amphitheater, bent forward and leering at a spectacle below.

The knife gleamed in her hand, and she licked her lips. The curved blade seemed a thing of shadow, but etched into the metal were runes that gleamed amid the dark. It felt good in her strong grip.

The mouth of Olekgar worked mutely, as though he still sought to voice some spell to thwart her. Fool. The Lethrin looked at her, the anger in his eyes a light as hot as the sun.

She moved to him. Slowly, like a lover's caress she ran the blade across his neck. A thin red line appeared. Then blood flowed, faster and faster. All the while he held her gaze, unflinchingly.

Next, she turned to Olekgar and did the same thing. He closed his eyes but his mouth still worked soundlessly, and to no purpose.

Blood spurted now from both sacrifices. Red, vivid, intoxicating to her as wine. She shuddered, and opened the wounds a little wider by the force of sorcery.

Crimson sprays erupted from pulsing arteries. Slowly, Olekgar collapsed to the ground. The Lethrin remained defiant, his eyes locked on hers until she reached forth with her hand and pushed him down. He resisted, but as life left him his body no longer obeyed his burning will.

She bent and drew a dark basin from behind her, and set it beneath the bleeding necks one at a time. The blood of the sacrifices mixed and swirled within it. The bodies were empty of life now, suitable vessels for what was to come. And though empty of life, the vestiges of their mind remained and would shape that which was about to enter into them. The strength of will as well as of body the Lethrin possessed would endure. So too the nimbleness of mind the acolyte enjoyed.

She ignored the bodies for the moment. What mattered now was their blood in the basin. She studied it, reveling at the sheen on its surface and the play of light within it that gleamed and glistened as the fluid congealed.

Ginsar breathed in of the night air. Power coursed through her and she laughed with the sheer joy of it. But her night's work was not yet complete.

She removed the basin from the corpses and sensed the eyes of the acolytes upon her, watching wide-eyed with anticipation. They knew what came next, for they had seen it before. Ignoring them, she turned her gaze to the thickening blood. This she stirred with her knife, shaping runes with each cut and stroke of the blade. Letters formed, and then dissolved back into the blood. But the power she drew forth slowly grew and took hold.

The air turned cool. An icy breeze stirred, sucking heat from those gathered there, and they pulled their cloaks tightly about them. The tendrils of mist creeping up from the river leaned one way and then the other as the breeze shifted direction.

Ginsar intoned words now as her blade moved through the blood. They were harsh and guttural, and as she spoke them she heard in her mind the voice of her master speak them also. Shurilgar had long ago taught her what to say, and it was as though he was in her head now, his voice one with hers.

She chanted more loudly, no longer muttering but boldly casting the words into the air. The knife handle grew hot to her touch, and the breeze turned into a gusty wind that tore the river-mist into shreds. The river itself churned and tossed in its banks, and a spout of water erupted high into the air with a cough.

And then there was more. Two voices rose in a chant of their own, and Ginsar felt the gateway between worlds tremble and the brush of something otherworldly on her mind.

"Come!" she commanded. "Come, for you are called!"

Vapor, red-tinged and wraithlike, rose from the basin of blood. The wind took it and cast it wildly into the air. And the two voices answered as one.

"We come, sorceress. We come, and your world shall be ours."

The blood in the basin caught fire, and Ginsar dropped it. The red mist formed around her, seeking entry into her body and she screamed.

The wind died. The river stilled. But the vapor churned around her, wrapping her in its dark intent. Fire dripped from her finger tips as she summoned her own power. Then she wrapped the mist within it, screamed once more as she tore it from herself, and sent it streaking into the corpses at her feet.

The acolytes scattered, fearful of falling victim to some stray tendril of magic. Even Ginsar felt panic rise within her, for she sensed the intent of the spirits she had summoned. They wanted to possess her, and nearly succeeded in doing so. Yet they had moved readily enough into the corpses when she forced them too, not bothering to continue to fight her. Why was that so?

The red mist clung to the two bodies, melding with them. After a moment, the corpses twitched and spasmed as renewed life entered them, changing them into their new forms. The Lethrin, or that which had once been the Lethrin, roared in pain and anguish. Almost, Ginsar thought, as if it still retained his defiance and hatred of her.

Ginsar stepped back. The acolytes dared come closer again to watch the transformation take place, to see the culmination of the dark magic even as they had watched its birth.

The bodies began to thrash. Skin tore where muscles swelled. Eyes popped and bones cracked, sharp edges showing before knitting together again in an altered shape. And then finally, the bodies stilled. For a moment they lay on the ground, and then slowly they rose to stand before her.

Her heart skipped a beat. Olekgar had become a Horseman. He was now Betrayal. Golden-haired he was, and beautiful. Tall and slim, his shoulders wide and his body athletic. Strength was in his every muscle, and they rippled beneath his fair skin. There was power in his blue eyes also, and they gleamed with their own inner light. Swift of movement he seemed, young and lively. But when he moved she saw knives in his back, blood constantly dripping from the wounds.

141

War was beside him. He was clad in armor, and possessed the full accoutrements of battle. In one mighty hand he held a great broadsword, saw-toothed and deadly. In the other was a shield of back iron, spiked in its center. A helm rested on his head, winged and cruel of visage. It too was of black iron, and a spike rose also from its top. A baldric of knives hung down his massive body from one shoulder to the opposite hip. And above his head fluttered two carrion crows that cried and cawed.

Ginsar raised her arms above her head. "We go to war!" she proclaimed to the acolytes. "We march tomorrow, and this I have learned from the dead. Brand comes to meet us." She smiled slowly. "Let him beware! We shall crush him, and all shall fall before us!"

20. You have Failed

The army moved forward for another day's march. Gil studied the country as he rode, aware that at any time an attack could be launched, and he and Brand would be its target.

It was hard to see much, though. Fog draped the hillsides, thick and eerie. Through it he caught glimpses of the lush forests that grew on the slopes. Everywhere was a potential ambush site, but he tried to trust in Brand's judgement that if one were prepared it would be in the gorge further down the trail.

He glanced over at Tainrik who now rode in the leadership group. The man was tough, of that there was no doubt. The surgeon had worked on him some time, properly cleaning and dressing his wounds, stitching the gash in his forehead that the scout had not been able to do himself and adding an infusion of herbs to the wine he sipped to reduce his fever.

And while the surgeon worked on him the scout had spoken with Brand and provided details of what had happened. Tough did not begin to describe him. It was not even a start, and Gil was sure he made light of some aspects that were the hardest and most difficult. It was the way of such men.

Brand had wanted to have him carried forward in a litter, but Tainrik had laughed. "Give me a horse," he told the regent, "and keep me awake so that I stay in the saddle. That's all I'll need."

Gil shook his head, amazed but at the same time proud. Tainrik was the sort of man that said little but achieved much. That was the best sort, and there were never enough of them but too many of the kind that spoke much and achieved little.

The scout looked better than he had last night, but still not well. When Brand had invited him to ride in the leadership group, Tainrik had joked that he had already risked his life, and survived. And now he was sure to be struck by an arrow fired from the fog and not even intended for him. Brand had just winked at him, and Tainrik had accepted the offer.

Gil considered what had been said as he rode. Loyalty was at the bottom of it all. It was the reason Tainrik had ventured out on Brand's request to look for the spies in the first place. It was why he endured so much. It was why he was here now, and not in a safer place of the army that was less likely to be the target of an ambush. The question was, how had Brand inspired such loyalty?

The regent never asked a person to do something that he would not do himself. He led like a true king, doing everything for the people and not expecting the people to do everything for him. He would have been like that as a captain also, when he had first met Tainrik. He was one of those few people who meant what they said and said what they meant. These were all simple things, but they were the hallmarks of good leadership, and Gil noted them.

Some while later they halted on a steeper stretch of road for their hourly break. Ahead, Gil saw the gorge. It ran between two high ridges that were smothered by a growth of forest and cloaked by shadow and the last vestiges of fog that had still not burned away under the long-risen sun. Just looking at it gave him goosebumps. The place reeked of danger.

Gil dismounted and saw Brand beckon him over. The regent led him a little way from everyone else.

"I have sent word back through the army that we expect an ambush here. They know that I have a plan, and that magic will be used. I have asked them, and now I ask you, to stay calm and act normal – no matter what you see."

"Of course," Gil said.

"And will you lend us of your strength? Of magic?"

"I'll help in whatever way I can."

"Then join the White Lady, and be ready to summon your power."

Brand moved away and retrieved his staff from where it was attached to his saddlebags. Then he wandered over to where Gil had joined the White Lady.

"Be seated," she said, offering Gil one of her most dazzling smiles. He had an inkling of an idea that she was going to enjoy whatever came next.

They sat upon the grass, looking out toward the gorge. "I'll shape the magic," she said, "but I'll draw on your power to do so. Summon it, and relax."

Gil allowed the lòhrengai within him to stir to life. It pulsed through his body, straining to break free as it always did, and he felt the joy of its presence but also the danger that too much use of it could bring. It was like a living thing itself, and it wanted to break free.

He sensed Brand to his right and the White Lady to his left. He felt also the summoning of their own power. The White Lady seemed different to him, her magic of a kind that he had not felt elsewhere. And it was strong, strong as iron but subtle also. But her mind was closed to him, and he gained no insight into her personality or purposes.

Brand was different. He too was strong, and though Gil sensed none of the subtlety of the White Lady, he felt the indomitable will of the regent, the unbreakable determination that had seen him survive struggle after struggle. He felt also the responsibility that weighed on

145

him. It was an immense feeling, made up of the lives of every single person in the realm, for every decision that Brand made could save or condemn them, and he knew it.

Separate, but also as one, their combined strength began to flow together. And of their power the White Lady formed an image. It was a glint of light at first, a stirring of fog and shifting of shadows. But it grew swiftly and took shape.

A wedge of cavalry headed it, for it was a replication of the army. Brand and Gil rode behind, surrounded by the Durlin. Then came the army itself. Nor was this illusion an image only, but each part of it moved and acted as though it were real. Gil was astounded by the skill that had produced it, by the seeming reality of it as it passed down the road and toward the gorge.

But the illusion did not come without cost. Gil felt the power drawn from him and the sapping of his strength. He began to breathe slowly and paid little heed now to the illusion. He concentrated instead on drawing forth his strength and keeping steady the bond between himself and the others.

The illusory army moved forward, and fog drifted down from a slope to obscure the real one, which had not moved. Gil felt a cold sweat break out on his skin and his concentration wavered. This was hard, but however hard it was for him it was more difficult for the White Lady. But he felt the joint determination of them all. To falter now was to waste their effort and fail to spring the trap, if indeed a trap had even been set in the gorge.

Deep down into the gorge the illusion moved, but nothing happened. There was no attack, no ambuscade and sudden flight of arrows and hurling of spears. It had all been for nothing.

The false Brand and Gil had nearly disappeared from sight when a burst of activity occurred. A hail of arrows filled the dark air of the gorge like a deadly storm. One struck Brand in the back, another pierced Gil's eye. All around them the white surcoats of the Durlin blossomed red. Screams rent the air and horses bolted. Bodies littered the ground, and a wild cheering came from men hidden on the ridges above the gorge.

But even as they cheered the bodies on the ground and the bolting horses and the survivors left milling around faded into nothing. Of the army, and the victory the ambushers thought they had won, there was no sign.

The mist around the real army dispersed, and silence fell. Brand stood, and into the quiet he spoke. By an art of lòhrengai his voice, neither loud nor soft, carried for miles around.

"Hvargil!" he called. "You have failed. And your treachery will catch up with you! Flee back to your outlaw den, while you can. And there wait, for you have set in motion your own doom this day. Cardoroth will no longer suffer you. We will come for you one day soon, and all we find with you."

Brand gave a signal and several hundred foot soldiers split away from the army to climb the rough terrain either side of the gorge.

The regent seemed tired, but he smiled at Gil. "They'll clear the outlaws out, if they remain. But they'll be gone before the soldiers reach them. They had thought to set an ambush and not fight a pitched battle. This was all a surprise for them, and I don't think they'll trouble us any further."

Gil nodded. "But you've done more than that. You always have an eye to the future. What you said to them will worry Hvargil. But it will worry his men more. And you did not threaten them, only him. All they have to do

147

to escape his doom is not be with him. I should think he will have less followers back at his camp tonight than he did this morning. And in the days to come more will desert him."

Brand reached out and placed a hand on Gil's shoulder. "You always were a quick student. What you say is true. We'll march back this way, and what I did will make it safer. And one day, you will have to go after Hvargil. You cannot allow his treachery to go unpunished, nor let him continue to incite treachery among the nobles. And the fewer men he has, the easier it will be to bring him to justice."

Gil knew that was true, but he did not like it. Hvargil was a relation, sharing the same blood and also a descendant of Carnhaina, just as was he.

Brand spoke again, but this time not to Gil. The generals were close by and they had heard his last words.

"You seem unhappy gentleman. Why is that?"

Gil gazed at them, and saw indeed that all three were scowling.

"Magic, Brand. It has no place in warfare."

The regent laughed. "You'd better get used to it. There'll be more before the battle is won, and most of it will come from the enemy."

That would likely prove correct, Gil knew. But was magic the real reason for the unhappiness of the generals? Or was it because Hvargil had been thwarted? He glanced at Brand, and sensed that despite his light tone he too was wondering the very same thing.

"It would have been better to just send troops as you did in the end anyway," Garling said.

Brand shrugged. "Perhaps. But then the outlaws would have merely tried again somewhere else. Now, they'll be disheartened. Perhaps even scared. Hvargil will sit back and await the outcome of the war with Ginsar. He will hope that Cardoroth wins, but in the process that Gil and I are killed."

He looked at Gil and winked. "We'll thwart that wish."

The rest break ended and the army commenced to march again. The gorge was secure, though it was slow going for the road was in ill-repair.

It was dark, with the ridges rising up to each side and the forested slopes blocking out the sky. The gorge was a menacing place, and Gil had the strange sensation that he had avoided death here. It was somewhere along the trail where he now rode that the ambush had been launched against the illusion. Arrows had hissed through the air and spears quivered in flight. It was a sobering feeling, and it brought home to him that he had enemies that wished him dead. That was not a good thought, but one that Brand had experience with, and Gil better understood the advice the regent had given him in respect of Hvargil.

They moved on, passing over ground littered by arrow shafts and spears. Gil shuddered at the thought of being here in the middle of the attack, at the very focus of it. Soon, however, the sense of menace passed and the gorge widened. The sky came out above and the sun shone once more. To Gil, it seemed a moment of rebirth and new opportunity. He was not dead, no matter what his enemies wanted. And he would make the most of that.

They were not quite out the other side when Brand unexpectedly called a halt. Whatever had disturbed him, Gil was not sure. But he felt a sense of unease himself, and a moment later understood why.

Sorcery. He felt it in his bones, and his own magic stirred to life in response. Just ahead, a slab of rock upon the road, perhaps toppled from the ridge above for it was cracked and fissured, began to exude smoke from its crannied surface.

149

The smoke, black and greasy, swirled and twisted through the air to form an image. In moments Ginsar stood there, beautiful and terrible as always.

"We meet again, Brand."

The regent sat relaxed upon his black stallion. "Only because I'm hard to kill, a fact that has taken you some while to appreciate."

The sorceress flashed him a smile. It even seemed genuine. "You *are* vey hard to kill. I know it better than most. But it's bad manners to mention my attempts on your life."

Brand bowed his head, but never took his eyes off the sorceress. "I apologize, lady. I'm only a rustic Duthenor tribesman."

"You're learning though," she said. "And I like that. Perhaps one day you would be at home in the throne room of Cardoroth."

"Ah, lady, you and I both know that isn't my fate. But, if you don't mind, time presses. What do you wish here?"

She shook her head. "So abrupt? The nobles of Cardoroth would never like that."

Brand did not answer, and Ginsar sighed. "I suppose you don't care much about the nobles. A pity, but never mind. What do I wish? Well, I want for nothing. I came here to tell you something, not to ask for anything. I know that you march to war and seek to surprise me. Did you really think to hide such a thing?"

"Ah, lady, did you really think that my purpose?"

Ginsar studied him. "You are quick on your feet," she said. "Another favorable quality, but you don't deceive me. I know exactly where you are, and where your army is. As well as your purpose."

Brand held his reins close and leaned forward in the saddle. "If you say so."

"I *do* say so! Come to me Brand, and we shall see just how good at staying alive you really are."

The sorceress turned to Gil, and he felt the power of her gaze. Evil she may be, and likely insane also, but there was a strength of will to her that he could not deny. And though she stood in the garb of a sorceress, with her dark boots tightened by silver buckles, her robes black and flowing, her cloak draped over her like a shadow, yet still she stood as proud as any queen and certain of her destiny.

"Savior or destroyer?" she said to him. "You will see soon enough which it shall be. I know the answer, as I know many things hidden from you. I know your true path, the fate and heritage that awaits you. Accept it willingly, for to struggle against it is futile. Destiny cannot be denied."

"You don't know my destiny," Gil answered. "And even if you did, I would not trust you to speak it truthfully."

Ginsar held his gaze for a moment, and then she sighed. "We shall see."

She turned then to Elrika, and Gil was surprised that she had spent little effort trying to convince him to believe her.

A moment Ginsar studied Elrika as though with curiosity, and then her eyes hardened. "Who are you to carry *that* sword? It was not forged for the likes of you."

Elrika did not seem cowed by the sorceress, and Gil was amazed at her reaction. She drew the blade with a hiss from its sheath, and held it before her.

"It may not be for the *likes* of me, but I would gladly use it anyway to spill your guts, hag."

Gil could not believe that she had said that. It was Shorty's influence on her he knew, for he heard an echo of the Durlindrath in them, yet she was the one who voiced them and his heart swelled with pride.

Ginsar's eyes blazed, but her answer was softly spoken. "You will regret that."

She cast her gaze over the others, ignoring the generals and lingering a little while on Taingern. Then her glance fell on the White Lady and remained there, transfixed.

"And who are you?"

"A secret within a secret. But you shall know soon enough. For now, think on this. To kill me is to doom yourself. To let me live, is *also* to doom yourself. You have overreached yourself, and there is no way back. The end draws nigh."

Ginsar was about to reply but the White Lady casually raised her hand and the image of the sorceress dispersed in a puff of smoke that drifted away on the breeze.

Garling was the first one to speak. "Are all you people mad? Why do you antagonize her so?"

"Better to antagonize her than fall thrall to her," Gil replied.

Garling shook his head. The other generals, Druigbar and Lothgern whispered to each other.

"One thing is clear," Lothgern said aloud a moment later. "Ginsar knows we are coming, that the army has left Cardoroth. Brand's plan has failed, and even as we speak the enemy may be hastening down the Halathrin road. If we don't turn back now, it will soon be too late."

A tense silence fell, but the White Lady broke it. "No. Ginsar's army is coming this way. I feel the Horsemen draw close. They and I are connected. And the sorceress acts in haste now, even as Brand had planned." She gazed at where the image of Ginsar had stood, her expression thoughtful. "Our coming could not be hidden from her for long, but it was long enough. She has summoned War and Betrayal earlier than she would have. She marches to a battle and not the siege she expected, and she is not one who likes to react to others. Brand has made her act in haste and change her plans. This is all to our advantage."

"More magic," muttered Garling. "All conjecture and intuition."

"We shall see," Brand answered. "But there is this too. She need not have revealed herself at all, and merely let us come. That would fit better with your view."

"Or she could be trying to deceive us," Garling said, "and make us *think* she is coming this way."

"She came," the White Lady said, "because she wanted to learn something. And she has, though by the time she understands what she has learned, it will be too late."

Gil hoped that was the case. But he understood where the generals were coming from. It seemed impossible just now to know what was true and what was false and what was going to happen. It was not a good feeling.

21. A Message

The next day the army of Cardoroth descended out of the hills and the forested ridges gave way to slopes of rolling grass. Scouts had been sent out during the night, and they began to return. By mid-morning they reported a massive army of elugs lay ahead. If Brand was relieved, he did not show it. Nor did the generals comment.

The scouts advised the size of the enemy. Their figures differed somewhat, but the averaged tally came to thirty-five thousand elugs and a thousand Lethrin. Against this, twenty-five thousand soldiers of Cardoroth would pit themselves. Small wonder, Gil thought to himself, that Brand showed no relief. Being right did not compensate for being outnumbered. And yet the elugs were not equipped as well as the men of Cardoroth, nor were they likely to be as disciplined.

Gil considered what he knew of military strategy. This was a great deal, yet it was all theoretical. He had never fought in a battle, let alone commanded one. Yet this was the golden rule: avoid engaging the enemy unless victory was certain.

The golden rule was easy to understand, in theory. Applying it was more difficult. What weight should he give to the elugs outnumbering the soldiers of Cardoroth? How should he assess the impact of the better equipment and greater discipline possessed by his countrymen? And what role would elùgai and lòhrengai play?

He could not measure those things, and he did not envy Brand who must. Nor could he weigh the greater strategy behind it all, which was to defeat Ginsar before she drew in too much through the gateway and gave the Horsemen power so great that they might usurp her. Any attempt to defeat her now must be a single and final role of the dice. To fail was to ensure no further opportunity arose. But if rivalry existed for the preeminence of a golden rule, it would come from this quarter: never stake success on the outcome of a single role of the dice.

No, Gil did not envy Brand at all.

A scout spoke to the regent even as Gil considered the situation. He had brought some new information and approached as the army rested.

"Are you sure?" Brand asked.

"Yes. Ginsar was seen, or at least a person who matches her description. Her acolytes were with her too. They are now encamped at the top of a large but gently sloping hill. It's a good defensive position."

"Very well then. Thank you for your good work. Best get something to eat and have some rest now."

The scout hesitated. "There's one last thing."

"Go on, then."

"I found the bodies of half a dozen scouts. They are not far from here, hidden away in a place where the road goes through some thick timber. They have been there some time."

Brand sighed. "Then they are the long-range scouts originally monitoring the enemy rather than any we have sent out in the last few days?"

"Yes, sir."

"Did you know any of them?"

"All of them, sir."

"I'm sorry lad. When we've done with this battle we'll retrieve the bodies and give them a fitting burial."

"Thank you, sir."

The scout left and Brand looked at Gil. "Hvargil has a lot to answer for. At least we know now why we didn't get word sooner about the enemy's movements."

Gil nodded. "You were right in what you said before. Hvargil must be dealt with, once and for all."

Soon after, Brand gave the signal for the carnyx horn to be blown, and the army marched again. It would not be long before the enemy came into sight, and it was possible that battle may be joined today.

Gil nudged his roan close to Brand's stallion as they rode. "Are we going to attack them?"

The regent pursed his lips. "We're outnumbered and they have the advantage of the land. On the other hand, the sooner we strike the better for us. We no longer have surprise, but the enemy, at least until recently, were not expecting a field battle but a siege. That is to our advantage."

Gil considered that. "This is all true, but you didn't say whether we would attack or not."

Brand gave a tight grin. "That's because I haven't decided yet. Best to see the enemy and the terrain first. It is not a decision to be rushed."

Later that afternoon, after marching many miles, both terrain and enemy were in view. The army of Cardoroth came to rest on a gentle rise opposite the enemy force. A mile of green grass separated them. It seemed peaceful now, with the sun out and a few white clouds drifting across a blue sky, but the threat of violence hung in the air and the green grass might soon be trampled red.

Brand rode a little way ahead, inviting the Durlindraths, Gil and two army officers with him. Gil studied the enemy, and his blood ran cold. This was a watershed moment in the history of Cardoroth, and what happened now, or soon, would shape the future.

He squinted against the angled rays of the afternoon sun and scanned the enemy formations. There was no cavalry, which was an advantage to Cardoroth. But after that, reason for hope was limited. In the center Ginsar and her acolytes were gathered. Sorcery would be used, of that there was no doubt. And there was only Brand, the White Lady and himself to defend against it. They were outnumbered on that front. And the numbers of the enemy as given by the scouts seemed accurate by his quick estimate. They would be better at that than him though.

On either side of Ginsar stood the Lethrin. They were few but they stood over seven feet, and though he had never seen them before, he had heard much. They were immensely strong and filled with an implacable hatred of their enemies. Folklore told that they were born from the stone of the mountains, and for all Gil knew it could be true. But irrespective of that, they were miners that hewed tunnels in the rock beneath their mountain homes with massive picks and unwearied arms. Because of their size and strength they usually formed the vanguard of elug armies. It was so here, and their mighty hands gripped massive iron maces, studded with spikes. To be struck by them was to die.

To either flank, like the unfolded wings of a great bat, were the seething masses of elugs: lank haired, ungainly, their dark skin tinged green. They were smaller than Lethrin, smaller even than men, but they were vicious and fierce fighters, never to be underestimated and especially so in large groups. They were prone to fleeing a battlefield, but they were also known to fight to the death should their leaders inspire bloodlust within them. If that could be done, Ginsar would do it.

"What do you think, Taingern? Should we attack?"

"There's no easy answer to that. But you know I'm cautious by nature. The fact that there's no plain answer

157

of yes suggests to me that we shouldn't. Not yet, not here."

"And you, Shorty?"

Shorty grunted. "No one has ever accused me of being cautious. My heart says to attack and get it over with. A delay will not change the inevitable. The enemy will always outnumber us. But still, Taingern may be right."

Brand looked back at the army officers. "What do you say, gentlemen?"

The first shook his head. "I agree with the generals. It would be best if we had the Cardurleth between them and us. We should not fight, but return to the city."

"And you?" Brand asked of the second.

The man looked a moment longer at the enemy, and then he met Brand's gaze. "You were right about Ginsar's strategy. She sought to come upon the city by surprise and besiege us. By marching the army out, you have confounded her plans and expectations. This is an advantage to us. As for the enemy army, I think that despite their superior numbers we can defeat them. But not by attacking uphill into their current position. We should wait her out. We have a direct route open to Cardoroth and supplies. We can delay. She, on the other hand, cannot. I do not believe the elugs are organized well enough to maintain food supplies over a lengthy period."

The man's view was interesting to Gil. It was something he had not considered before.

"And you, Gil?"

"I think we should wait. It will force her to move against us, especially if the enemy is not as well organized as we are."

Brand rubbed his eyes. It was a sign of uncertainty and anxiety, and one of the few times Gil had ever seen him reveal either of those states of mind. After a moment the

158

regent nudged his horse a few feet ahead. By himself he studied the enemy in silence a little while longer.

Gil sensed the weight of responsibility he must feel. It was enormous. But even as Gil watched, Brand lifted his head a little higher and his features became set. He had made his decision.

The regent turned his horse around and trotted back to camp. The others followed. They dismounted, and Brand issued instructions to the army officers. "We'll camp here," he said. "Send out sentries at full strength. I also want roving bands of cavalry further out, to ensure we have good warning should the enemy move."

"Yes sir!" the two men said in unison. They made to leave, but Brand stopped them.

"One thing more. We shall dig a trench and throw up an earth wall. Set the soldiers to digging immediately."

The two men saluted and Brand turned once more to study the enemy. Gil looked as well. He could see Ginsar, recognizing her by her height and the acolytes all around her, yet keeping a reverent distance. They worshiped her, but they feared her also.

"So," Gil said. "We're going to wait her out, try and see if we can force her to attack us."

"Is that the impression you get?" Brand asked.

Gil was confused. "Well, we're obviously not going to attack. Otherwise we wouldn't waste the effort of the men in digging defenses."

Brand winked at him. "Maybe. Then again, in warfare the aim is to ensure the enemy believes anything, anything at all except the truth."

The regent moved away to speak to the commander of the sentries. Gil was stunned and did not follow. Were they really going to attack this afternoon? Or would Brand rest overnight, and then try to surprise Ginsar in the morning?

159

What remained of the afternoon passed swiftly. The enemy did not attack. Nor did Brand. The earth rampart was built after much labor, but many hands made light work as was often said in the city. Tents were erected, and horses and pack mules tended to and fed. Night fell, camp fires sprung up and the scents of cooking filled the air.

But even as the camp began to settle down after dinner was eaten, Brand was issuing orders. Gil saw him speak to several commanders. They saluted swiftly, and when he came back to the command tent and rejoined them all Gil asked him what was happening.

"War," the regent answered.

A cold chill ran through Gil. "You mean that we're going to attack now? At night?"

"What is the one thing that an army must do if it is to win a battle?"

"It must outfight the enemy," Gil answered.

"Many would say that, but it is not so. The one thing an army must do is *outsmart* the enemy. Strategy is everything, and without it courage and skill and determination wither like unharvested grapes on the vine. Strategy is the master of war, and deception is always the goal until victory is obtained."

"Then if we're not fighting now, but the men seem to be decamping, does that mean we're returning to Cardoroth?"

"The men are moving, but you will note that it is being done quietly and under cover of dark. The roving cavalry will keep enemy scouts away so that Ginsar should not discover that we have left until daylight. We will be gone by then, and be out of sight. But no, we're not returning to Cardoroth."

"Really?"

"No, but Ginsar may believe so after what we have done this afternoon. She will think that perhaps we received news from Cardoroth. Maybe a revolt of the nobles and another attempt for the throne. She will not know, but she will seek to work out why we came all this way, established a camp and then left despite all expectations. An emergency back in the city is the best explanation, and she will consider that possibility most carefully."

"Could she not discover the whereabouts of our army by magic?"

"Perhaps. But if she does…" Brand glanced at the White Lady.

"I will prevent her, should she make such an attempt," the White Lady announced.

"The enemy scouts will be key," Taingern said. "They must not be allowed to follow us or to discover that we're not returning to Cardoroth."

"Precisely," Brand agreed. "The roving cavalry have instructions to that end. And, to ensure Ginsar believes what I want her to, I have a plan."

"What plan is that?" Gil asked.

"The simplest of all," Brand said with a faint smile. "I'll leave her a message."

22. We March!

Ginsar woke to the gray light of dawn and a fading sky of stars. She loved the night, but the pinprick of a million lights ruined the perfect dark. She did not like that, and suddenly she knew that if it were it in her power she would burn the stars to ash.

She sat up. Strange. She had not always hated the stars, but that version of herself that liked them was long since dead. Yet still, she knew that she had changed more recently too, and it made her uneasy. Could she really burn the stars to ash? From whence had that thought come? And was such power even possible?

An acolyte approached. She felt elùgai stir within her. If she could not yet destroy stars, yet still she could burn this creeping sycophant…

With a wrench of will she calmed herself and let her power subside.

"Mistress," the acolyte said, bowing low.

"Speak!" she commanded.

The acolyte kept his head down, not looking into her eyes.

"They are gone, Mistress."

"Who has gone, worm?"

"The enemy, Mistress. They left during the night. Their camp is empty."

Ginsar stood and fury was in her eyes. The acolyte fell to his knees but she ignored him. Instead, she looked out over the long mile of grass that separated the two encampments. The fool was right. Brand was gone. The army of Cardoroth was gone. There was nothing there of

162

the enemy save the dirt ramparts they had constructed, dim and shadowy in the muted light.

But Brand would not leave. No, not him. There was no give in the man, and he would fight to the last breath without stint. Yet the impossible had happened. He *had* retreated.

She turned to the acolyte. "Worm. What do the scouts say?"

The man groveled on the ground before her but answered. "They don't know what happened, Mistress. Many have failed to return and those remaining report they have found some of their comrades dead. The enemy made sure the scouts did not get near enough to see what was happening."

Ginsar gritted her teeth. They were all fools. It was the purpose of scouts to monitor the enemy by stealth. They should not have been found and killed.

She allowed herself a small smile. One day, she would have a better army than this. Bigger. Better. This was but the beginning of…

The urgency of the situation pressed itself upon her. "Fetch my horse," she instructed the acolyte. "And gather the others."

The man scrambled away and she tried to calm herself. She considered the destruction of Cardoroth, of the sacking and burning of the city. The smoke would rise high into the sky. She had never seen the funeral pyre of an entire city before. That would be something new.

After a while she grew more tranquil, and the acolytes arrived mounted on their black horses. One led her own mount forward, but it was not black like the others. It was milk-white. Long ago, as a child, she remembered her father had given her a pony colored in the same manner. She had loved that pony.

She crushed the memories of her past. They would not help her. She mounted the horse and kicked it forward into a trot. The others followed and they left the army behind.

The grass flowed beneath the hooves of the horses and some sense of privacy returned to her. She hated being crowded in by the army, so many eyes looking at her when she was not looking at them. So much noise as well. This was no substitute for the secrecy of her dark forest, yet it was better. But soon they came to Brand's camp, and she looked around warily.

It was deserted, and had a sense of utter abandonment. The earth ramp set up a perimeter, but nothing was within. Deciding to walk rather than risk injury to the horses by jumping the trench and clambering up the loose soil, she dismounted and left her horse with the acolytes to hold. She brought only three of them with her.

They crossed the rampart and strolled through the remains of the camp. All about them the ground was rutted by wagon wheels, hoof marks and the tread of thousands of boots. The grass was mostly gone, trod into the earth and killed. In the air hung the smell of animal manure and the scent of smoke from the campfires that were stoked up and allowed to burn through the night long after the enemy had gone.

The sun was well up now, and its light glinted from a sword driven into the ground. It was the one thing out of place, the one thing left when all else was taken. Why?

Ginsar saw that attached to the hilt was a leather strap and she paused. What did it mean? But there was only one way to find out.

She gestured to the nearest acolyte. "Fetch the blade."

The man moved away warily, perhaps fearful of some trap of magic set by Brand. But there was none. She would sense it if there were.

Hesitantly, the man approached. He studied the blade momentarily, then cautiously reached down, grasped it and drew its point from the earth.

He returned and handed it to her. Glancing momentarily to the blade she saw that it was of no importance. It was an ordinary sword such as some common soldier would carry. She removed the leather strap and cast the weapon from her.

Burned onto one side of the leather were several words. *We will not surrender.* She knew they came from Brand, and she read them to the others. "What does it mean?" she asked them. "Why has Brand gone?"

"It makes no sense," said one. "They came here to fight."

"It makes sense to me," another said. "They have seen our army now, and they know they cannot beat us. They have returned to hide behind their walls of stone."

"And what do you think?" Ginsar asked the third acolyte.

The man hesitated, but he answered after a moment. "I don't know, Mistress. Brand would not give up … and yet he is gone. Is it a ruse of some kind? Perhaps. Or maybe he had news from the city of a revolt. You have certainly planted the seeds for that."

"What kind of ruse?" Ginsar asked.

"One to make you leave the superior ground that you have and fight him on more even terms."

"It could be," she said. "Yet why the message? It is so much like him to fight until the end. But why feel the need to tell us? Unless perhaps he had news of a calamity of some sort over and above our army. I think he wanted me to know that no matter what, he would not give in."

She stood in silence a moment, considering. The acolytes had not added anything that she had not thought of herself. They were of little use to her, and as always she

165

must bear the responsibility of making all decisions herself. So be it, she thought.

"Well," she said eventually. "We'll not find out standing here all day. Wherever the enemy has gone, and *why ever*, it makes no difference. I'll follow them and destroy them! We march to war!" She strode toward her horse, but called out over her shoulder. "And send out more scouts!"

23. All things Die

Gil sat on a camp chair, slowly sharpening his sword. The rasp of the whetstone cut the air, and he worked with methodical strokes, honing the best edge to the blade that he could. But though his hands were busy, his mind was free to wander.

He looked out beyond the camp. They were in the last of the hills. Or the first of them. Everything was a matter of perspective. But what mattered most was that they defended the route back to the city, and that the landscape was lightly forested. This offered concealment for the army.

"Here come the cavalry captains," Brand said.

The regent was sitting beside him, enjoying what had been a momentary break from the constant stream of decisions and reports. But Gil knew he was waiting on the cavalry report with eagerness.

The three captains saluted.

"What news, gentlemen?"

One of the men stepped forward a pace and answered. "We found many elug scouts during the night. They were all killed."

"Good work. And what about since dawn?"

"A new wave of scouts came out from the army. There are many of them. Fewer now, of course. And we are keeping them at bay. They have not yet slipped close to our position and cannot suspect where we are."

Gil put down his whetstone. "Would Ginsar not deduce our position though by the fact that we are killing her scouts? Wouldn't that indicate we're hiding here?"

"It might," the captain replied. "On the other hand, it could just as easily be taken as normal practice. A retreating army doesn't want the enemy coming up too close behind it."

"Exactly," Brand said. "It could be either, but we can do no more than hope our message convinced her and that she thinks we're returning to Cardoroth."

Gil knew that was true. Brand had rolled the dice, but there was no word yet if the ploy had worked. Their own scouts had not yet returned.

"Good work, gentlemen," Brand said. "Please pass on my commendations to your men. They've had a long and sleepless night."

The captains saluted and left.

Gil watched them depart. They and their men had done a difficult job well, and he felt once more the stirring of pride. The citizens of Cardoroth were good people, but they were often let down by their leadership. He would soon, if Cardoroth survived the coming battle, be in a position to do something about that. He would continue Brand's work of promoting people on merit rather than aristocratic connections.

But that was a problem for the future. First, they must live. He sat back in his chair and glanced at the regent.

"Do you think Ginsar will come after us?"

Brand rubbed his chin. "I don't know. But I *do* know this. Either she will or she won't. Which it will be, I can't control. But, if I had to guess, I'd say she fell for the bait and is even now marching this way."

"I think so too," Gil said. "And it might be a good thing. Our soldiers are now resting and the elugs will reach here after a march. They'll be less fresh than us."

They sat for some while longer in silence. The camp was quiet around them, for the men rested. They had marched hard and fast overnight, but they had come to a good defensive position, and they had blocked the way through to Cardoroth. Ginsar could not go around them except by taking a long route around the hills.

Within the hour though fresh news came to them from the cavalry. Ginsar had indeed left her defensive position and was proceeding toward them.

Brand acted swiftly. He ordered the army to decamp from the thin forest in which they were concealed and into the open. He explained his tactics to Gil as they moved forward.

"We could remain hidden," he said, "but the enemy would be suspicious of terrain that could hide an army and that their scouts were prevented from entering. Ginsar would not march into a trap, and we would be in a stalemate for no purpose other than delay."

Gil had guessed as much, and he knew also where Brand favored the battle to take place. As they came out of the trees they reached a long slope of grass and Brand signaled a stop.

The gradient was not especially steep, but it advantaged the army of Cardoroth over the enemy. That advantage was not so great, however, as to cause Ginsar significant concern. Given her superior numbers she may well attack anyway. At least Brand would hope so.

"The intent is to engage her," Brand said. "We may force a victory here by our greater skill and discipline. I think we will. And I think, having been tricked to leave her own chosen field of battle, she will be angry. She will attack us."

Gil felt unease in the pit of his stomach and his palms were sweaty. He knew a fight was coming, one such as he had never seen before. Brand seemed unconcerned though. This was a mask however, and Gil knew it.

Brand gave instructions. Flags were used to communicate, and horns also. The army soon formed its fighting position.

The front ranks were bolstered by picked regiments of doughty fighters. These were men who had fought before and proven their courage and skill in battle. The left flank was left to the cavalry. They could play a decisive role, for the enemy had no cavalry of their own.

Behind the ranks of the infantrymen were archers. These would fire over the heads of the squatting men before them until the enemy drew close. Then the infantry would stand, lock shields and form a shield wall to halt the advance of the attacking enemy already decimated by the barrage of arrows. So much, at least, was the basic theory. What would happen in reality was yet to be seen. He was not even convinced that Ginsar would attack, though his nausea and sweaty palms told him otherwise.

Brand and the leadership group remained at the rear of the army on a higher part of the rise with a good view of the situation. The Durlin were all around them, but despite their position of relative safety, it would not last. Soldiers liked to see their commanders fight, and fought better themselves when that happened. Brand would at some point do so, and Gil made his own decision in that regard.

The enemy was now visible. They marched toward Cardoroth's army and halted less than half a mile away. Their array was as it had been previously: in the center rode Ginsar and her acolytes, while to either side of Ginsar stood the Lethrin. Then, forming the long outer wings to each side were the great masses of elugs. They milled about with little discipline, and they were short, ungainly and fidgety, but that did not mean they would not fight well.

Both armies were still, tension rising between them like a storm that might discharge a lightning bolt at any moment.

Ginsar was seen to make a sign, and from the ranks behind her four horsemen, cloaked and hidden, rode out. One came ahead, taller and larger than the others, and the remaining three followed. These were her heralds, though Gil had an uneasy feeling that they were more than that. No doubt Brand sensed it also, but he called Gil forth to come with him, and Taingern and Shorty also.

They rode forward to meet the heralds at the halfway point between armies. As they neared, Gil saw just how large the lead rider of the enemy was. He was massive, and not a man at all but a Lethrin. Gil had never heard of that race riding before. Nor had he seen a mount of such size either. It too was massive, and its black eyes had a dead look to them.

The two groups came to a stop some ten feet apart. The first enemy rider reached up with a gauntleted hand and pushed back his cowl.

"I am War," he said. His head was protected by a great helm of wrought iron, black as midnight and ornamented with cruel wings. On his arm was strapped a shield. It too was of black iron, spiked in its center. Armor he wore over his massive body, spiked and scaled. And a sword hung to his side, a massive blade that seemed as though it could fell trees, and that the rider possessed the strength to wield it so was apparent.

A black cape hung over War's mighty shoulders, and this seemed to catch the breeze and quiver. Yet Gil realized that it was not so. Two crows fluttered into the air from behind the rider and wheeled above his head.

Brand paid no heed to all of this. He sat relaxed in his saddle. "I'm Brand, leader of those who oppose Ginsar."

171

War inclined his head gravely. "Of you, I have heard. And I wonder why you lead the rabble behind you to destruction. But perhaps you do not know there is a choice. Kneel before me now and swear allegiance. You and your army may join us, and we shall conquer the world."

Brand's black stallion grew restless, but the regent patted his neck and calmed him. "And to whom would I swear allegiance? You or Ginsar?"

War laughed, the sound muffled by the great helm. "You know the answer to that, warrior."

"Indeed I do. And you should know that I will not forsake Cardoroth, nor Alithoras. I will fight, and so too will the army behind me."

War answered, and his voice betrayed neither anger nor surprise. It was merely cold. "Then you shall die, and every soldier in your army also."

Brand did not seem perturbed. "All things die."

"Not I. Nor my companions."

War made a gesture and the three riders behind him came forward. One by one they removed their hoods. The first was a young man, and his face was bright and his eyes clear. Golden-haired he was, and tall and slim. He moved with the grace of the warrior born, and his muscles rippled beneath well-tanned skin. Yet as he moved Gil saw knives in his back, blood constantly dripping from the wounds. It was Betrayal.

The next that Gil looked at was no living man. Where a head should have been there was only a skull. Tufted hair sprouted from it. Skin clung to it in patches and hung loose in others. Maggots fell to the ground from squirming orbs where the eyes had once been. Yet though no eyes were left, still the orbs, writhing pits of horror that they were, locked on Gil's own gaze. This was Death,

172

returned to Alithoras though previously defeated by Brand.

Gil knew what he would see next, but turned to the last rider anyway. He seemed a tottery old man. His back was twisted and hunched, his eyes red and rheumy. His gnarled hands trembled with palsy, and the skin that covered them was thin, hanging like ragged cloth from little more than bone. But power was in the man's gaze, power that took the breath away. For this was the horseman Time. And he too had once been defeated.

Gil's mind reeled. How could they defeat an enemy that returned from defeat itself?

He glanced at the regent, and saw there was a tight smile on his face. "I shall repeat myself," Brand said. "All things die. No matter their strength. The good and the bad alike. Those who desire death and those who do not. Even worlds grow cold and spin into dust. Tell your mistress we do not surrender. Or rather, tell your slave."

War inclined his head. With no further word he turned away and beckoned the other horsemen to follow. A few moments Brand watched them go, and then he rode back to the army in silence. There was nothing to say.

Once there they took up their positions on the rise above the army once more. Brand called Gil and Elrika to him.

"The battle will begin now. I want the two of you to stay close to me, and to each other."

They both nodded solemnly, but neither answered. At that moment the enemy charged. Across the grass one half of their army raced, churning it into dust as tens of thousands of boots pounded the ground, and the drumming of their footfalls and clash of sword on shield sounded as thunder.

"Ginsar is a fool," Brand said over the tumult. "There was no need to charge until they came within range of our bows. It serves only to tire a soldier before battle is joined."

"And why hold part of her army back?" Gil asked.

"This is but a test before the day is done, and she does not care how many soldiers she loses. She will wait until tomorrow to come against us in full, and she does not think she can lose."

Wise or unwise, the enemy rushed toward them and the thunder of their coming was a noise Gil would never forget. Perhaps the fear of it was another reason why she ordered an early charge, and he was not so certain that Cardoroth's soldiers would stand against the enemy. There might not be a tomorrow.

As the enemy came within range a new noise sounded. The foot soldiers of Cardoroth kneeled. Behind them the archers drew their bows and sent forth a great volley of arrows that blackened the air and hissed like an angry wind.

Elugs fell. Some were killed by arrow, others merely wounded. But all died as the great army surged forward treading over those who fell and churning the earth red with their blood.

On the enemy came, and another volley of arrows thickened the air. More than a dozen times this occurred, and it took a dreadful toll upon the elugs. At the last, the bowmen withdrew and the spearmen cast a shivering mass of javelins that hit the enemy like a wall.

The enemy faltered, for the javelins were heavy and thrown with power. Yet after the wounded fell momentum reasserted itself and the charging army surged on.

Now, the foot soldiers of Cardoroth stood. The first rank stepped forward a pace and locked their shields together into a wall. They did not fight as individuals, but as a unit of men. Shields on the left, a short sword stabbing forward on the right above the wall or through small gaps to the next shield.

The two forces crashed together in a horrendous clash of weapons. Screams and battle cries tore the air. Blood sprayed. And men and elugs died.

On the elugs came, a mad rush of them climbing over their dead and attacking in a mad fury. They wished to win, to defeat the men of Cardoroth in the first rush and sweep them into oblivion. Under the fury of the assault the front line of Cardoroth gave way a little, stepping back against the onslaught. And many of them died. But as they fell others stepped in from behind plugging up the shield wall once more.

The line buckled, but did not break. Then, slowly and surely, the line straightened and formed an impenetrable barrier. The momentum of the elug charge was lost, and now they died in greater numbers.

Far away and dim, Gil heard a horn blow. It was the signal for retreat and had come from the enemy leadership. The elugs, attacking in a mad fury one moment turned and fled the next. Away they streamed, and clouds of arrows followed them. It was the price to pay for retreat, because shields held to the front did not protect against arrows in the back.

The space between the two armies was empty now, save for the dead and dying. Brand sat upon his horse, and strain was on his face. Gil thought he would signal for a charge of his own, that he would counterattack now that the enemy had retreated. But the regent let out a slow breath and smiled grimly.

"The sorceress made an error, yet it was not so great as it seemed. Nearly I went after her, but her force still outnumbers ours, and she has not yet committed the Lethrin nor the Four Horsemen to the fight. This she hoped I would do, and then we would face our greatest

175

enemies while at the same time giving up our advantage of ground."

"I thought you would," Shorty said.

"And I also," Taingern agreed.

Brand relaxed. "I nearly did. And perhaps we would have won too. But perhaps not."

They watched as stretcher-bearers went out and assisted wounded men. At the same time soldiers moved out onto the field retrieving arrows and javelins. But they came back soon as a stir went through the enemy.

Gil strained to see. "Something is happening, but I can't see what."

Brand also was looking hard, one hand shading his eyes from the sun. "She is sending the Lethrin now, I think. I expected her to wait until tomorrow."

In a few moments Brand was proven correct. A thousand strong the Lethrin stepped forth. They did not run yet, for they were better disciplined than the elugs, or else Ginsar had learned from her previous error.

They formed a wedge, pointing themselves at the men of Cardoroth, and it was clear what they would attempt. Using their strength and momentum, they would pierce the shield-wall of Cardoroth's soldiers and drive through the ranks. Then, the elugs would follow. Should that happen, they would win the battle.

The Lethrin wedge moved forward. Behind them several thousand elugs gathered, less disciplined perhaps, but if the Lethrin broke through the shield wall the elugs would pour through after them, widening the gap and ensuring it could not close. Then Ginsar's whole army would charge.

The marching pace of the Lethrin grew into a trot as they approached. And as they came into range of the bowmen they broke into a run. At that moment Brand ordered a flag signal given. It was an instruction to the cavalry.

Cardoroth's horsemen streamed forth from the left flank. They were positioned here for they were right handed, and they carried long and heavy spears. This was their weapon in a charge, and they streamed forth, spears ready to strike the enemy to their right.

Each of the cavalrymen also carried a curved sabre for fighting in a melee when their spears would not be useful. But their role here was to use the speed of their charge and the added power that gave them to harry the Lethrin. That, no doubt, was Brand's plan. But Ginsar had foreseen it and the elugs behind the Lethrin would have the role of protecting the backs of their massive companions while they tried to break through Cardoroth's shield wall.

The Lethrin wedge hurled toward the men of Cardoroth, and the stamp of two thousand booted feet rumbled over the earth like thunder. Arrows darkened the sky, and the hiss of their flight was as a sudden gust of wind. The storm was about to break, and Gil felt the fear of the men on the shield wall. Could they stand against such a charge as this?

The volleys of arrows had little effect on the Lethrin. Their skin was tough like the stone from the mountains in which they had been born. Yet here and there one fell, stricken in the eye or neck. More succumbed to the javelins. But not enough. They could be killed, but not easily. On they came, mostly unaffected by the hail of missiles, and they smashed into the shield wall.

Screams tore the air. Men died and the Lethrin fell upon Cardoroth's soldiers like a hammer blow. Where they hit, the line dissolved, the first rank falling as wheat beneath a scythe. So too the second rank. And also the third. But the charge of the Lethrin slowed and men fought them now. They died, but the Lethrin died also.

Gil watched in horror. There was so much death, and the Lethrin were mighty beyond the ability of men to combat. Yet still the men fought, and working together they brought down their great opponents gradually. But it would not be enough.

"Watch!" called Brand, and his arm swept out to point at the cavalry. Gil had forgotten them, transfixed by the Lethrin, yet now he looked further back.

The cavalry neared the rearguard of elugs. These had turned and prepared to fight, but at the last moment scattered and fled before the charge of horses. Few were the warriors who had the heart and skill to stand before a mounted attack.

The elugs raced away, leaving open the way to the back of the Lethrin wedge. The horsemen thundered toward it, spears held high in their right hand, guiding the horses with their left hand on the reins and their legs.

With a battle-cry that tore at the sky and rose above the clash of war, the cavalry struck. These spears were not for throwing, but long and heavy, and driven by the momentum of the horses they pierced the stone-like flesh of the Lethrin and killed them by the score.

The first of the cavalry to hit them rode past, and the next in line had their turn. Yet Gil watched as the first riders began to wheel around. They would ride in a circle, keeping a constant and deadly pressure on the Lethrin.

The rear of the Lethrin wedge was forced to turn and fight the cavalry. This stalled their forward momentum. The battle raged on, and some of the Lethrin, though impaled by spears, leapt forward in their death throws and dragged riders from their mounts.

Gil looked at Brand, and he saw the regent was pale-faced, and his fingers white on his clenched fists.

Brand did not take his eyes off the battle, but he spoke. "Watch Ginsar," he said. "What matters now is that she does not act swiftly."

Gil looked out over the battle to the enemy ranks in the distance. He saw movement there, and picked out what he thought was Ginsar's tall figure among the acolytes who milled about her. Intuitively, he knew exactly what Brand meant. If she acted decisively and ordered a charge against the cavalry she could disrupt their attack on the Lethrin. But had the tactics of mounted spearmen caught her by surprise? She would likely have been expecting them to use sabers or perhaps light bows. Neither would have been greatly effective against the Lethrin.

The battle drew Gil's eyes again. The Lethrin continued to press forward despite their losses. The shield wall wavered, beginning to buckle backward. There were not enough men to keep coming forward and fill the gaps left by the slain.

Garling stalked over to Brand. "Send reinforcements, fool! Or we are lost!"

"No," Brand said, turning his cold gaze on the general. "Ginsar is waiting for that. If I peel men away from the flanks, she will attack. We would not turn her back then."

"If you don't, then we are lost anyway. Once the Lethrin are through our army will flee!"

"You are wrong, general," Gil said. "These men have courage! Look and see!"

Even as Garling debated the matter, the men of Cardoroth rallied. They did not panic. They did not flee. They changed their tactics and men came forward with javelins. These they did not throw, but rather used them as stabbing weapons, driving forward with their bodyweight behind them.

The Lethrin, assailed on all sides and suffering heavy losses, gathered in close together and attempted a retreat. But that was a fatal error, for now that the men of Cardoroth saw that they had the upper hand they redoubled their efforts. Between the ranks of infantry and the cavalry, the Lethrin were slain to the last man. He went down with a great bellow and three spears through him.

The cavalry wheeled away and returned to their position on the left flank. From the whole army erupted a mighty sound of yelling and cheers. They had survived. They had defeated a charge of Lethrin, which few armies had ever done. It was an act of defiance against death, and an act of defiance against the enemy who wanted to overrun them but had failed.

Garling said nothing. Gil looked at Brand as the sun sent westering rays of red light across the sky as it set. "Will they come at us during the night?"

The words were addressed to the regent, but it was the White Lady who spoke. "No. But tomorrow will be bad beyond your imagining."

24. The Prince!

Gil slept poorly. There was much noise from the army as they celebrated into the night, singing and cheering. And the words of the White Lady proved correct; no enemy attack was initiated through the night. Yet her other words haunted him: *tomorrow will be bad beyond your imagining.*

He rose in the predawn light, unrested and worried. He dressed, and then donned his cumbersome mail shirt and a plain helm. He had one of silver, decorated and inlaid with threads of gold, but should the worst happen it would not prevent a sword from splitting his skull any better than the plain one.

He met the others in the main room of the tent. They were somber. Each one of them knew that the battle would be won or lost today. Each one of them knew that they might die. They also understood that if they did not defeat Ginsar, tens of thousands of innocent people would be slain, and the city razed to the ground. Somberness was appropriate.

There was no speech from Brand. There was no attempt to lift their spirits or distract them from the situation. "Good luck to one and all." He said simply. And he meant it. That was enough.

They moved out of the tent, and Gil felt Elrika's hand clasp his own. "Good luck," she whispered into his ear.

Despite the movement of men all around the camp, there was a stillness in the air. The last stars faded from sight, and the leadership group took up their positions on the rise above the army of Cardoroth.

The sun rose. It had set as a fiery ball of red light the evening before. Now it slipped above the horizon, golden and bathing the east with a pale glow. The sky gradually turned blue. The grass became green and the air was fresh upon Gil's face. It could be his last day to see and feel such things, and he looked about him at the wonder of the land.

But the elug army had its own view of the world, and it was nothing like his. Over the gulf of trampled grass that separated the two armies a single drum began to beat. And then the chanting of the enemy began. The cruel words had been heard outside the walls of many besieged cities before this, and on open fields of battle too. The words carried to Gil, and he knew and understood them. He feared them also.

> *Ashrak ghùl skar! Skee ghùl ashrak!*
> *Skee ghùl ashrak! Ashrak ghùl skar!*

The chant flowed, seemingly without beginning or end. The drum hastened. Stamping boots thundered, swords clashed against shields, and dread thrummed through the air.

> *Death and destruction! Blood and death!*
> *Blood and death! Death and destruction!*

Thus chanted the elugs, and their dark words seemed to fill the world and block out sun and sky and grass. But Gil straightened even as he heard them. He was the son of kings and queens, and he would not be bowed by the dark.

His hands clenched into fists and his eyes shone. This was a day like no other, and it seemed that his whole life had hurtled toward it. Afterward, he would be dead. Or he would become the king his people needed.

182

Beside him Brand gave a signal. A score of carnyx horns sounded. The men who bore them were tall, and the bronze horns matched them foot for foot. The soldiers held them high, the mouths of the instruments twelve feet above ground, and from their metal mouths issued an unearthly moan that sounded like an otherworldly beast.

The elug army gave a final roar, and then they rushed forward screaming. None were held back this time, and everything hung now on the outcome of this final battle.

It was no measured charge that surged across the field toward the men of Cardoroth. There were no marching ranks, no phalanxes, no shield walls. What came against them was a surge of screeching enemies, waving swords and clubs, a primaeval wave of destructive hatred.

As had happened before, the front ranks of Cardoroth's army knelt and the archers behind them unleashed swift-flighted death. Elugs fell in writhing heaps to the ground but the rest came on. Now javelins tore into them, but still the enemy rushed forward, screaming their hatred and heedless of their slain comrades.

The seething mass crashed against the shield wall. The men of Cardoroth stood their ground. Gil glanced along the line and saw that everywhere a wave of elugs hit it, sought to tear it down, and died in the attempt. Yet the mass of elugs kept clambering forward. The air seemed like a crimson mist while blood sprayed and spurted. But the shield wall held and the enemy spent themselves against it.

Nevertheless, they still came on and the men of Cardoroth grew weary. When the captains could, they signaled by whistle for the front rank of their units to fall back and the next rank to step forward. But moments of respite were few.

The elugs gave no quarter. The men of Cardoroth did not expect it. This was a fight to the death and only one army would walk from the field.

"There," Brand pointed. "The line is bucking."

Gil looked to the right side of the battle where Brand indicated, but saw nothing. But the regent was proved correct, his eye for battle keener. In moments, Gil saw it too. The shield wall began to give way. Yet even as he watched the soldiers of Cardoroth rallied and pressed forward once more.

Brand looked over at him. "Do you feel it?"

"What?"

"The malevolence. Sorcery is being used. It empowers the enemy and weakens us."

Gil realized it was true. It was something that had been on the edge of his consciousness, but subtle enough that it did not bring attention to itself. Perhaps it came from the Four Horsemen, but more likely it was Ginsar's work.

The line showed signs of buckling again in the same region as before.

"Shall we use magic of our own to oppose her?" Gil asked.

Brand shook his head. "Not of the sort you mean, but of another kind. Between Ginsar, her acolytes and the Horsemen we are outnumbered. We must preserve our magic for when we need it most. Courage is called for now, a means to give the men heart."

Brand was about to ride into battle to rally the soldiers, and Gil knew it and understood why. But he reached out and put a hand on his shoulder.

"No. They have seen you fight before in other battles. But they have not seen me. And I am their prince, their king to be."

Gil tightened the strap of his helm and then mounted his horse. Without another word he galloped down to the line on the right side. There he handed his reins to an archer and drew his sword.

A cold thrill ran through him. There were no Durlin now. No guards. No protection. This was a battle, and this was what it was to look death in the eye. But he was needed here, and without facing death a man cannot live.

He pushed forward, and his voice rang out above the clash of battle. "Hold the line, men of Cardoroth! We'll teach these elugs to fear us for a thousand years!"

They were not the finest words he had ever spoken, but they had the effect he wanted. Some of the men in the rear ranks turned and looked at him. And they knew who he was.

A cry went up. "The prince!" some called. Others yelled "Gilcarist," using his full name. More heads turned in his direction. More men called out, rallying to his name.

He pressed forward, and the soldiers let him through. Before he realized it, he was at the front and a man died before him, his throat torn out by a curved elug blade and bright blood spilling onto the trampled ground.

A soldier from the second rank jumped into the gap, holding back the swelling tide of enemies that sought to overrun the defense.

Gil bent down and swept up the shield of the dead soldier. He ran his left forearm through the straps and fixed it in place. Then he drew his sword. It was a longer blade than the soldiers carried, meant for swordfights rather than the simple jabbing use of a shield wall, but it would do.

Around him men called out. "The prince! The prince!" The cry was loud now, taken up by many mouths, and it surged behind him when another man died a little to his left and he leaped forward to take the dead man's place.

Gil stood in the front rank now. His shield was up, locked in close to the man at his left. Against him came a

185

wave of elugs, all snarling faces, hideous cries and bent swords slashing. Gil felt a blade smash into his shield, felt the weight of the elug trying to bear him back. His sword jabbed out. The elug screamed. Blood gushed from his groin. One of his own kind pulled him down and leapt into the gap. He brought a club to bear, a massive thing of gnarled timber, and it heaved through the air at Gil's feet.

Gil lowered his shield. It blocked the blow, but his head was now exposed. A second elug slashed at it, but Gil ran him through. The first elug heaved high his club again, but the man to Gil's right jabbed a sword into the side of his neck. The elug screamed, and in turn went down like the one he had replaced moments before.

The battle went on. The sound of sword striking shield and the screams of agony and hate filled the air. But Gil noticed it less than the stink of death, of opened entrails and the pungent odor of urine. This was battle. This was death, and for all the horror his mind went swiftly numb. All he knew was block and jab, but some small part of his mind also knew the line was being pushed back and would soon buckle again.

"Hold!" he cried. "Hold for Cardoroth!"

All about him he sensed the desperation of the men. They were tired and weary, sick of death. But they gave just that little bit more of themselves. And the tide turned. They pressed forward a few steps. The elugs washed against them like a spent wave now, the surge of their hatred sweeping along to another part of the shield wall. For the moment, this section was in less danger of being overrun than others.

Gil stepped back when he could and a man behind him slipped seamlessly into his place. All around him men cheered. They knew it was his first taste of battle. And he had survived it, becoming one of them in a way that nothing else could ever achieve. Suddenly, he understood better why these men loved Brand and trusted him, and why the regent in his turn felt the same way.

He cleaned his bloody sword on his trousers, for he had no other means of doing so, and nearly vomited. Then he made his way back through stretcher-bearers carrying dead and wounded men. He came to his horse, where the archer who still held the reins clapped him good-naturedly on the back. "If we survive this, you'll make a fine king," the man said.

It was the sort of thing that no one would ever normally say to a prince, yet it was not out of place at this moment.

"We'll survive," Gil said. He swept his arm out toward the ranks of soldiers. "With men such as these, how can we lose?"

He nudged his horse into a trot and made his way back to the leadership group. He felt their eyes upon him: grim but proud.

He dismounted, and silently Elrika handed him a rag. He took it and looked down at his sword arm. It was slick with blood. He knew his face was spattered red as well. He nearly vomited again, but instead rested his shield on the ground and methodically cleaned himself as best he could without water. He looked again at Elrika. She did not speak, but returned his gaze with somber eyes.

The regent broke the silence. "The blood of your line runs true," he said. "You did well. The shield wall would have collapsed had you not buoyed the warriors."

"Battle is fickle," Shorty said. "Minutes ago we faced defeat, but now we hold strong and the enemy throws all their might against us without success. Perhaps we should advance and attack them in our turn. We might route them just now."

Brand considered it, but then slowly shook his head. "It's too early. We have yet to see the Four Riders enter the fray."

The White Lady stirred uneasily. "It will not be long."

25. Day of the Durlin

The battle raged on. The elugs swarmed against the shield wall, but they did not break it. It weakened though, and at times Brand went down to fight. At other times Gil returned to the fray. Each time the soldiers rallied and held off the enemy.

In Gil's mind, the cold fear of defeat and death still had a grip, yet slowly the thought crept into his mind that Cardoroth could win the battle. Against an enemy who outnumbered them, they had held their own. And the elugs died in greater numbers than the men did. The tide had begun to turn with the destruction of the Lethrin, and it kept flowing now in Cardoroth's favor.

But no sooner had he begun to hope for triumph than a dread seeped into his very bones. A sense of wrongness wrapped itself about him and infused the air.

"It begins," the White Lady said. "See there, behind the battle the Four Riders are moving?"

"I see them," Brand answered. "And I will go to meet them." He turned to Shorty. "Will you come with me?"

"I wouldn't miss it."

The regent looked at Gil. "It is not wise for both of us to battle at once. You must stay here. And you Taingern as well. I leave you both in charge."

Taingern nodded. Brand and Shorty prepared to ride down to the lines, and the White Lady spoke. "Not all is as it seems, I think. But the Horsemen are moving, and I feel them prepare some sorcery. I must oppose them." She looked at Gil. "Be careful, young prince. Your hour is coming soon."

She mounted her white horse and they rode down to the back of the army. The three of them would oppose the Four Horsemen, and Gil thought he should be with them. But though the Horsemen had moved, they had not yet entered the battle.

Tainrik watched them go. "I think I'd better help," he said.

Gil was not sure that the scout was well enough to fight. But loyalty to Brand drove him, and it was not Gil's place to stop him. "Be careful," he advised.

After they had all left, a cool wind began to blow. Gil paid it no heed, but after a while it turned very cold and his unease stirred. The horses, tethered close by, stamped their hooves and flicked their ears. Then the wind died and the air grew deathly still. A white mist gathered on the ground and sent wavering tendrils upward.

"Sorcery!" Gil cried, and the skin on the back of his neck tightened. He went to draw his sword but discovered the mist was about him and had suddenly tightened like chains cast over his arms and body. He could not move. He felt the magic within him come alive, but it fluttered and died down again as though some influence of the mist dampened it like water on fire.

It was then that he saw forms within the swirling mist. They rose upward, groping figures of terror driven by dark magic. Drùghoth they were called. Sendings. He remembered their description from Brand's teachings and what they were capable of.

He could not move, chained by sorcery as he was, but he could see. The drùghoth came for him, rising up like dead men from earthen graves and lurching in his direction.

But Taingern was suddenly there, and beside him Elrika and the Durlin. To his surprise the generals also

190

sprang into action, drawing their swords and standing between him and the sendings.

Dozens of wraithlike creatures pressed forward, and the vaporous fog eddied around them. The creatures glided on tall legs and their long arms reached forward like creeping fingers of mist. Worst of all, the drùghoth had faces: gaunt, cold-eyed and cruel. A pale light lit their hollow cheeks and glimmered silver-white in their trailing hair.

Taingern leaped toward them and yelled the battle cry of the Durlin: *Death or infamy!* Elrika was only a step behind him and then the Durlin and generals charged as well.

Taingern attacked. His sword sliced and cut and stabbed. The sendings were more solid than they appeared, and Gil heard them cry as the Durlindrath's sword bit into them. So too with the other defenders. Yet though the wounds drew forth shuddering screams, yet their cries came as though from a great distance, and the creatures did not die. Instead of falling, they came on, slowed but not deterred.

Gil struggled to free himself from the sorcerous chains, but the cold of them bit through his flesh and stilled his magic each time. He watched in horror as Durlin after Durlin died, sacrificing their lives so that he had a chance to live.

One of the drùghoth slipped between the thinning ranks of guards and came for him. Gil saw his death in the creature's pale eyes as it reached for him, but suddenly Elrika was there, the ancient sword in her hand flashing.

Three times she struck it. The sending shuddered and screamed, but did not die. Then with a wicked slash of its clawed hand it struck her back, raking long nails across her left side and sending her spinning.

Once more Gil tried to summon his magic, but failed. He knew he must try something new, and instead of summoning his own power he reached forth with his mind into the surroundings. He felt the fog roiling about him, thick now, billowing like a cloud, but beyond it was something else. Beyond the sorcery he felt the warmth of the sun, and he felt that he could use that.

Elrika stumbled, but she righted herself and swept her blade at the drùghoth's legs. It lurched back, and Gil felt the sun and drew its warmth to him.

Light flared. The fog rolled back. With a trembling movement, the magic within Gil stirred once more. It became one with the light of the sun, the sunlight one with it. Then Gil summoned all his will and let fire burst from his body.

The sorcerous chains fell with a screech like tortured metal and then hissed away in a cloud of steam. Gil drew the magic to his hands, feeling the marks on his palm throb, and he lashed out at the creature struggling with Elrika. It screamed, and then fell apart and drifted into the thinning fog.

Gil scattered his magic around him, feeling it grow and expand, feeling it obliterate the sendings and burn off the last remnants of fog. When he was done, he drew in a breath and let the magic falter. Looking around, he saw the devastation that the sorcerous attack of Ginsar had wrought.

Only he, Taingern and a handful of Durlin still stood. Elrika lay sprawled on the ground close by, blood smearing her clothes. He felt a sense of dread, and was about to go to her, but instinct warned him that the attack was not yet over.

The last of the fog hissed away in a puff of steam and a wave of heat rolled over the bloodied grass. A figure shimmered, tall and ethereal. At first Gil thought it was Ginsar, but as it took form he realized it was not. This was a thing of nightmare instead.

It was a summoning of fire, standing some ten feet tall and towering above the men who stood there and watched it in awe. Smoke rose from beneath its cloven hooves. Ash fell from it in a shimmer whenever it moved. Its eyes burned and shifted like pools of molten metal, white-hot and deadly. In its giant hands it gripped two swords that flickered like tongues of red flame. And the head was crowned with curved horns that sparked fire from their tips.

The summoning took a step forward. Taingern moved to block its coming, and the handful of Durlin gathered behind him.

"Stand not in my way, mortal."

The voice of the summoning throbbed like the bellows of a furnace and smoke curled from its flared nostrils.

"Leave this place," Taingern answered. "It is defended."

The creature looked down on him. "You cannot defend against such as I. Flee, or I shall send your soul to an eternity of burning pain and agony. Flee!"

"Eat dung and die," Taingern said quietly.

Gil had never heard Taingern speak like that. And he saw that the man trembled all over, but also that he did not step away.

The menace of the summoning was a palpable force. The air was alive with it, and it grew. Gil felt the pressure of it, felt a primal fear so strong that he worried it would still his heart. It beat against him in waves, and he saw the Durlin fall to their knees, overcome. So too did he fall.

But not Taingern. The Durlindrath had stood his ground against threat and sorcery both. Not only that. His sword was in his hand and he leaped forward to attack.

The twin swords of the creature flashed through the air, cutting arcs of fire. Taingern dodged and ducked, then

193

leaped high and rammed his own blade into the neck of the summoning.

With a howl of sparks and smoke the creature wheeled away. But it lashed out with its blades again. They whistled through the air like lashes of fire. Taingern leaped and ducked, coming at the thing with courage and skill. The blades sought him out. He dodged and weaved, smaller and more agile than his enemy.

Several more times the Durlindrath hammered home blows to the summoning, but nothing stopped it. Taingern's white surcoat was scorched and smoldering, but he himself had avoided contact with his enemy's blades.

But it could not last. Almost like a dancer Taingern moved about his opponent, spinning, withdrawing, leaping in to attack. Yet one error would see him dead.

The error came. Taingern ducked left to avoid a massive blow. He was about to step in and deliver another strike but the creature had foreseen his intent. With a heave of its giant body it kneed the Durlindrath and sent him flying to land on the ground several feet away. There he lay, his sword fallen from his grip, and though in great pain he tried to rise.

Stepping forward, the massive summoning trod on him, smoke billowing from the cloven hoof. It came on toward Gil then, and Taingern lay still behind it.

The remaining Durlin tried to rise, but they did not have the strength of will of their leader. The flaming swords of the creature cut them down. Gil watched, stricken to the core of his being and wondering if death would be a merciful release from what he had seen. Everyone had died to try to protect him.

The creature moved toward him. In his wake, he left tread marks of singed grass. With horror, Gil realized that Elrika lay before him. She might be dead, but even so he could not allow this abomination to trample her body before it killed him.

Some flicker of defiance stirred within him. It rose up, and it contended with the dark sorcery that weakened his mind and body. The creature drew closer, a massive and ponderous thing whose shadow darkened the ground.

Gil remained terrified, but he staggered up and came between the summoning and Elrika. Like a pillar of shadow and flame the thing stood before him, and it heaved high both its flickering swords.

Time slowed. Gil sensed death hover above him, but from behind the summoning there was movement. Somehow Taingern had risen. Blood soaked his surcoat, but he staggered forward and reaching upward thrust his blade into the back of the creature's neck.

The summoning howled, but not even this was a killing blow. It spun around, knocking Taingern backward with one arm. The Durlindrath went flying, but landed and rolled groggily to his feet. The creature strode toward him.

Yet in the howl of pain that the thing had vented Gil heard hope. It had not been a cry of the creature, but rather it was the combined voice of many men sounding as one. And finally Gil understood the nature of the sorcery. It was not a summoning, but a creation of dark magic, made of the thought and directed by the purpose of Ginsar's acolytes. This was how they had pinned him down and held him in chains. Together, they were too many for him. Defying the creature, the sum total of their power, was too hard. But one by one would be a different thing.

His sword was of no use to him, and Gil let it drop to the ground. He held high both his palms, and from them he allowed his own magic to flare. Tendrils of power shot forth and wrapped around the creature. But it was not an attack.

195

Gil worked quickly. He felt the nature of the creature, sensed its powers and from what it had been made. Lastly, and most importantly, he found the thin trail of sorcery that commanded it from afar. He concentrated and dived deep into the feeling that gave him.

His body slumped to the ground and he felt it no more. But as a glimmer of spirit and magic he raced down the trail of sorcery and into the midst of the acolytes.

The acolytes sat in a circle, chanting. In the center of the circle he formed an image of himself, clad as a warrior with a sword that glittered like starlight. It was made of his memories of the constellation of Halathgar, which was fitting because it was the Sign of Carnhaina, their deadliest enemy, and he was her heir.

The chanting faltered as they saw and knew him. But it was too late. He leapt among them, sword flashing, wreaking death and destruction with a cold fury he had never felt before. They died swiftly as they tried to rise and flee, the last thing they saw being the blaze of his eyes and the glitter of his starry blade.

He sensed the fire creature back in his camp billow away into sparks and smoke as the sorcery that sustained it died. Casting his eyes about he saw the dead bodies of the acolytes, but of Ginsar there was no sign. It was foolish, for she was stronger than he, but he wished she were here so that he could challenge her, stronger or not.

One of the acolytes moved to Gil's side. The man tried to stand and flee, but Gil's anger was not spent. The glittering sword in his hand flashed. Blood sprayed and the man's head toppled from his body.

Gil looked around once more. The acolytes had chosen a place to work their magic that was distant from the battle. He saw it now from the other side, and he wondered what damage he could do appearing behind them. But he felt his strength fade also, for the magic he had worked came at a price. All magic did.

Weariness flooded through him. The sword faded away and so too the image of himself that he had made. In spirit form he fled back to his body.

Back in the camp his eyes flickered open. He scrambled up to a standing position, but swayed with dizziness and fatigue. Looking around he saw that Taingern knelt on the ground, gasping and pressing his hands on his ribs. Some of them must be broken from the weight of the creature stepping on him. All around him were the dead bodies of the Durlin. And the three generals also. They could have fled, but had not. They were better men than he had thought, but he would never be able to tell them so now.

He heard a groan behind him and turned. Elrika was struggling to her feet. She had survived! A flood of relief washed over him, but with it came a towering anger. Ginsar had wrought this destruction, and she would pay for it. He swore it would be so, no matter the cost.

26. This is the Hour

Brand, Shorty and Tainrik stood in the first rank, playing their part in the shield wall. They fought side by side, the enemy falling to them, the men around them rallying. It was at this point that the Four Horsemen directed their malevolence, and all about him Brand sensed the fear of the men. But they did not succumb, would not succumb while he was there.

A little further back he sensed the White Lady. She had invoked her own magic, and it spread through the ranks of Cardoroth's soldiers. It shielded them from the worst sorcery of the Horsemen, though she was careful to mute their power only, rather than confront them. That time was close, he felt it drawing on apace, but it was not quite here.

A wave of elugs rolled up against the wall. Their hate-filled eyes gleamed, madness glinting in them. The Horsemen drove them on, lashing them into a frenzy with their sorcery, and the elugs, even when wounded to death and their entrails spilled upon the earth, still crawled at their enemies and tried to stab their feet.

"For Cardoroth!" Brand yelled. And though the men around him were near to panic, yet still they fought by his side and did not retreat. Moreover, the longer this went on, and the more the enemy threw themselves against the shield wall with all they had, yet failed to break it, the greater grew the confidence of the men.

The line that had been buckling straightened and the fury that drove the elugs lessened. Still they were driven by sorcery, but their fear was growing for sorcery could not blind them entirely to the destruction wrought upon their own army. The frenzy of their attack subsided.

Within the midst of the enemy horns sounded, and Brand knew their purpose. It was a retreat. Ginsar had thrown everything against them and failed. Soon would come a reckoning. The army of Cardoroth now outnumbered the elugs, and the spirit of victory infused them.

The elugs streamed away. The hiss of swift-flighted arrows followed them, killing them as they fled. Brand withdrew from the shield wall, and Shorty and Tainrik joined him. Blood spattered the scout, and some of his stitched wounds bled again.

The regent shook his head. "You should still be resting, old friend."

"Time enough to rest when we've won," Tainrik answered.

The White Lady interrupted their conversation. "I'm sorry, Brand. The push by the Four Horsemen was a ruse. They are yet to unleash their full power, but while we were occupied, the enemy has struck. Somehow, Gil has survived the attack."

Brand felt a chill within his bones. Everything depended on Gil, and he had left him alone. Quickly he strode to his horse, mounted and galloped back up the slope. The others followed close behind.

He saw Gil from a distance. But all around him were bodies. The enemy had wrought havoc, and dread settled over him.

As he drew closer, that dread intensified. There were few survivors here. Smoke coiled from dead bodies, and he knew the Durlin were dead. All of them except for Taingern. And he looked badly injured. Brand could tell from a mere glance that he had broken ribs.

Brand reached them and leapt of his black stallion. He took in the scene. The stench of sorcery still hung in the air, but he felt lòhrengai also. Somehow Gil had found a way to beat opponents that were stronger than he. The prince seemed angry, an emotion that Brand had rarely seen on his face. But Brand understood why. Yet there was relief too, for Elrika had survived as well as Taingern.

The prince turned to him. Anger burned in his eyes, but there was a coolness too. In that moment he reminded Brand of Gilhain, the old king. The blood ran true in his veins.

"It is time to attack," Gil said softly.

Brand answered solemnly. "It shall be as you wish, Gilcarist. And we will make them pay."

He turned then to Elrika. "I don't know what happened here, but I see that your wounds are to the front and not on the back. You earned the sword you carry today, and he who bore it first would be proud of you. For today, you are a hero worthy to walk by his side. And in the days to come, you shall also be a Durlin. If you wish it."

The girl turned her gaze to Gil. "I wish it," she answered.

Brand put a hand on Taingern's shoulder, but he had no words for him. It was Taingern who spoke.

"They gave everything they had," the Durlindrath said.

Brand knew who he meant. He looked at the dead Durlin, men that he had known and worked with. They were his warrior brothers. "We will avenge them," he said to Taingern.

They mounted their horses then. Even Taingern. The broken ribs would hurt now, but he could still fight and would not hang back. Tomorrow, he would be barely able to move. But by tomorrow victory would be theirs, or they would all be dead.

Brand withdrew his staff from where it was tied on his saddle bags. Battle was coming now, and one of magic as well as blades. The purpose of the White Lady was drawing to fulfillment, and so too Gil's destiny.

They cantered back to the army, and Brand gave his orders. Signals were issued, and the cavalry set upon a charge. They thundered off from the left flank to sweep their spears across the enemy.

The elug army had retreated, but they had not fled the field. They were in disarray though, and the cavalry, on reaching them, killed and scattered many in the front ranks as they passed.

Brand watched as the cavalry pivoted neatly on the other flank of the army and swept across them again. This attack was not so successful. Many of the riders' spears were broken, and the men fought with their sabers. This brought them into closer combat with the enemy and some were killed. Also, the elugs had brought forth their archers. This too began to cause devastation.

Brand signaled for the cavalry to retreat and return to the flank once more. At the same time he also signaled for the army to march. It was time to attack.

As a single unit, the men of Cardoroth pressed forward. They did not run, but marched. The shield wall came first, locked in a long and impenetrable line. Behind them the other ranks.

When they came within range of the elug bows they marched at a faster pace. The shield wall did not alter, but the ranks behind lifted high their shields to form a roof. Against this a hail of arrows fell, volley after volley, yet few men were injured or killed.

The elugs possessed no javelin throwers, and soon the army of Cardoroth crashed into the enemy. The elugs hacked and slashed, fighting with fury and wild strength.

The men of Cardoroth held the shield wall together and relied on discipline.

Screams tore the air. Once more men and elugs died. Brand signaled, and the cavalry galloped out again, but this time they went to harry the enemy from the rear and cause confusion. It was the price Ginsar paid for not having cavalry of her own.

The two armies were locked together now. Cardoroth did not advance, nor the elugs retreat. And death continued unabated.

Brand moved into the ranks, but he remained mounted. The others followed him, forming a wedge. "Forward!" he cried, and the men heard and saw him.

The soldiers of Cardoroth drew of their great courage and fought with all their might. Slowly, ever so slowly, the shield wall advanced. Brand came to the front of the line and he used his staff as a spear. Elugs leapt at him, but his great stallion reared and tore at them with his hooves. Upon his back Brand swung his strange weapon. An elug went down, blood running from an ear. Another fell, his head snapped back by a thrust from the end of the staff. The great stallion trampled both.

There was space about him now. The elugs feared him, moving away. Taingern and Shorty rode beside him, their swords slashing. Tainrik and Gil likewise. So too Elrika, but Brand noticed she stayed close to the prince, protecting him as best she could.

The mounted wedge penetrated deeper into the enemy ranks. The elugs began to panic and chaos reigned among them. "Forward!" cried Brand again.

"We come! We come!" came the answering roar from the men of Cardoroth, and the shield wall advanced more swiftly.

The White Lady was among the mounted wedge also. She did not fight, nor was she attacked. She rode as

202

though unseen, and there was a mask of determination upon her face that gave Brand pause. Something was afoot, and even as he realized it she called out to him. "To the left! Strike to the left!"

Brand smashed an elug away, feeling the thrum of contact jar his arm, and angled his horse as she had advised. Then they all saw what the White Lady had sensed. War was there, and the other Horsemen also. Of Ginsar there was no sign, but Brand knew she would be close.

He raised high his staff and allowed his magic to flare. Light flickered about him. "I come for you!" he cried, and pressed forward. The elugs gave way, and War turned his own steed toward him. A challenge had been issued and accepted.

They came together. The battle raged all about them, but a space opened for the two combatants. War swung his great broadsword, saw-toothed and deadly. It moaned as it cut the air, and red fire glinted on its edges like sparks of blood.

Brand deftly guided his mount back. Yet even as the horse moved he thrust forward with the staff. White fire burst from its tip and ripped into the Horseman. His black helm glittered with light and sparks flew from the spike at its peak and flowed down the vulture-like wings of its side.

War shook his head and laughed. But massive as he was he moved swiftly, feinting with his sword and then pressing the rim of his black shield with the side of the blade. The wicked spike in its center detached and sprang forward with great force.

Brand summoned lòhrengai again, forming a barrier before him. The missile struck it and bounced away. Quick as thought Brand let the force dissolve and nudged his mount forward. He struck with his staff, bringing it down in a whipping motion against the sword wrist of the enemy.

War cried out, moving his mount to the side. The two crows that fluttered above him screeched, flapping madly in the air.

What their purpose was, Brand did not know. But he did not trust them and guessed they may be used as a weapon. He sent a blast of fire into them and they burst aflame, sparks showering down onto War. Then they fell to the earth, two bones that were not those of birds but looked like sun-bleached ribs.

Brand readied himself to attack War, but the Horsemen kicked his mount forward and the beast charged, smashing into Brand's stallion. Brand nearly fell, but righted himself in time to see the great broadsword hammer down. But it was not directed at him. Instead it bit into his horse's neck, near severing it.

The horse screamed and toppled, blood spraying from one of the great arteries. Brand leapt from it, barely escaping being crushed as it fell and kicked in its death throws.

Brand felt a surge of sorrow. Tears sprang into his eyes. That horse had been dear to him, had been with him since his first days in Cardoroth. But there was no time to mourn; War came for him, his own steed jumping the dying horse and his great sword raised high once more. It fell over brand like the shadow of doom.

But though Brand was disadvantaged, a man on foot facing a mounted enemy, he would not allow himself to be beaten.

The great sword swung down. Brand shifted left and ducked below its deadly sweep. Then, gathering his legs beneath him, he leaped high. He did not try to strike with his staff. Rather, he thrust it in front of the rider while he landed behind him. There, he nearly fell, but he got his knees under him and found purchase atop his enemy's mount.

With a deft move, he gripped the other end of the staff with his left hand and pulled it up beneath War's black helm. War sensed what was coming, and he elbowed backward with his sword arm. The massive elbow struck Brand and winded him, but his enemy could not reach him properly to deliver a full-strength blow.

Brand pulled the staff as tight as he could, and then he allowed himself to fall back off the horse. In this, War's steed helped him for the extra rider jumping onto his back and then toppling caused him to rear.

It almost did not work, but Brand was a large man and his weight, though nowhere near that of the Horseman, was enough to pull them both down from the horse.

They fell in a ruin of tangled limbs, and Brand had to roll to avoid the weight of his enemy crashing atop him. He lost his grip of the staff with one hand, but kept it with the other. Scrambling away he stood up.

War was just as quick to his feet and the speed of his opponent's movement surprised Brand. Nothing that big should be able to move so fast.

The other three Horsemen moved forward. Brand took this as a sign that they thought War vulnerable. Seeing them, he could not help but wonder how Ginsar had brought the two defeated ones back. At what risk to the world had she done so? And what would she risk now?

He knew he would soon find out. The sorceress stepped from behind the riders, defiant and determined though her army was being swept away around her.

Defeat was imminent, yet she did not seem anxious. He admired her then, but he feared her also. Now would come the great moment of this conflict. Now she would seek to draw greater power through the gateway to aid her and stave off her downfall. Now, Gil would come into his inheritance and the purpose of the White Lady would be revealed.

And even as he watched, he saw Ginsar begin to chant and felt the power of her sorcery thrum through the air and sink into the very earth.

Gil felt the White Lady close beside him. "Now, prince, is the hour come for which you were born. This is the time of your great choice."

Her words were true. Gil felt it, but he still had no idea what he would do or what was expected of him. The White Lady had told him once that he would know when the time came. But he knew nothing.

The battle raged on, moving away from this island of a battle within a battle. He sensed Ginsar invoke her power, and he heard the harsh thrumming of her voice as dark magic filled it. The gateway between worlds was opening like a spinning vortex in the sky above the field of battle. Ginsar widened it, began to draw more force through from the other side.

Gil looked at War. He could tell the Horseman sensed the same magic at work, or at least the thing summoned into the body of a dead Lethrin did. He felt the Horseman's anticipation, even yearning for what was about to happen. Gil did not know what he was meant to do, but he understood that he could not allow Ginsar to continue.

The great battle of men and elugs receded. Brand and the Horseman were stilled as though their fight was no longer of significance. And into that momentary peace Gil strode. He did not raise his sword, but instead summoned the power of lòhrengai. It burst into life inside him.

Ginsar turned to him. Her eyes were alight with her own dark magic, and there was no surprise on her face.

She had known this moment was destined, and perhaps knew better than he what it meant.

"Come to me, my prince," she said.

"Never," he answered. "Turn away from your intention. Do not open the gate wider, or we shall all be lost."

She gazed at him as though considering his words. "I was born lost," she said. "As were you. Elùgrune they called you. And they did so for good reason. You were born to be one with the dark. Embrace it, and know peace. Embrace it, and the power that it brings. It is like nothing you have ever felt. Come to me!"

"No. You tried to kill me a little while ago, and now you place the world in jeopardy."

She smiled at him. "I did not try to kill you. That was my acolytes, and you gave them their reward. You are greater than they were, greater by far. Nor would I ever truly hurt you. I understand who you are." She swept her gaze over the others and lingered on Brand before fixing her eyes back on him.

Gil felt unease surge through him. "You know nothing of who I am."

"I know this," she answered. "They would make you nothing but a mere king. I, on the other hand, would teach you sorcery and give you your heart's desire. *Magic.* It is your birthright as much as kingship. I would make you a sorcerer king. Nor would I let you settle for a stinking city full of vagabonds and traitors. Not I. Instead, I would guide you to rule other cities … other lands. A king? Nay. You would be an emperor!"

Gil felt the call of his magic then. It *was* his heart's desire. Being king was a duty, and one that he had never wanted. But magic could make the world a better place. He could achieve so much more with it than he could as a king. Yet he had no wish to conquer other lands, no desire to be a king at all, much less an emperor.

"No," he said. "You don't understand me in the least."

Within him his magic stirred restlessly. He still did not know what he would do to stop her, but if needs be he would attack her and try to kill her. Even as he thought it, he knew that she was vulnerable now. Perhaps that was why she was talking to him. She would not like to risk taking her will and power off the gateway to defend herself, or the opening would begin to close again.

Ginsar tilted her head. "I do not understand you? How wrong you are. I understand you better than anyone else in the world. Shall I tell you why?"

Gil did not give an answer. But Ginsar needed none. Slowly she raised her hands. Gil saw then what he least expected – two pale marks upon her palms, twins to his own.

"I know you, Gil. I understand you as no one else ever could. We share the same heritage. We possess the same blood, and verily, the same magic from days of old before the first stone of Cardoroth was ever laid."

Gil shook his head, stunned. "It's not true."

"True? Are you so wise as to determine truth from lie? I do not think so. Not yet. But I am not lying to you. I am of the same line as you. Even as Hvargil is. Why else do you think he has my favor? We are all of the same ancient blood. And blood calls to blood. Come to me, Gil. And I will teach you the mysteries of the universe."

The world seemed to stand still. Everything that Ginsar said rang with truth, but he could not believe it.

"No," he said, a third time. "It cannot be."

"It is. And it is good. You know me as Ginsar. But once, long ago, I was Ginhaina, sister to Carnhaina from whom you descend."

She held him then with her gaze. And he stood, transfixed by her revelation. Blood *did* call to blood, and he felt the kinship with her. He also sensed the great depth of time that separated them. She was born long ago. She was the daughter of the first king of Cardoroth. Who was *he* to judge her? Who was *he* to know the truth of events from so long ago?

"Come to me!" she commanded.

Gil did not know what to do. He felt the gaze of everyone upon him, and most of all Elrika by his side. He thought of the time he spent with her in Carnhaina's secret library. He felt who he once was and who he wanted to be.

"I will say it again, Ginsar. The answer is no. I will not join you. But if you wish, you may join *me*. Close the gateway. It will destroy you. But I will stop the Horsemen, one way or another, before that happens."

The sorceress looked at him. A moment she stood still, as if in doubt. Then she shook her head.

"Fool," she said regretfully. "You could have had it all. Now, you will have nothing. You cannot defeat me. The power is in me now, a part of me. It is beyond your strength. And I protect the riders. Even if you had the power, you could not send them back. We are one now, linked by forces you do not understand."

But Gil did understand. The Horsemen were bound to her, for she was their anchor in this world. She protected them, fed them strength. But she was also bound to them by the same force. It was a closed circle of magic. But...

A new realization came to him. The White Lady was drawn through the gateway too. She was balance. They were all bound together, and they could not exist apart. If she went back to her own world, the others would be pulled through with her. But for her to go back, the body she had in this world, the physical form that she had

209

incarnated herself into, must die. It was made of this world, not her own, and could not pass back with her.

Suddenly, the White Lady was by his side and she whispered in his ear. "Do what you must, Gil. It was never a choice between savior and destroyer. You are both. To save all you love, you must destroy me. I cannot do it by myself."

Gil's mind swam with the enormity of the choice before him. The Horsemen were called into the world by sacrifice. Only sacrifice could send them back. Only the death of the White Lady...

27. I have Failed

Ginsar screamed. Her wail rose, high-pitched and keening over the battle field. When it ceased, her eyes blazed. "No!" she said. "I will not allow it." But Gil was not sure to whom she spoke. She could not have heard what the White Lady had said.

Even as he hesitated the Four Horsemen advanced on Ginsar. They moved neither swift nor slow, but with a unified purpose. And he sensed a greater vigor about them. The spell the sorceress had begun was starting to work, but already the Horsemen had too much power and were beyond her control.

One moment the Horsemen moved, and then the next their bodies collapsed. A terrible stench of corruption filled the air, but four clouds of red vapor rose from the crumpled corpses and shot like arrows at Ginsar.

The sorceress shouted defiantly. The red vapor enveloped her, pouring into her through nose and mouth and ears. She screamed once more, this time in agony. And she began to change. Her face and body twisted and contorted. At one moment she took on something of the appearance of War, but he in turn was overthrown by Death. So it went through all the Horsemen, all vying to possess her and control the others, slipping down and rising up again in turns as they struggled. But another visage appeared also: dark of hair, grim faced with wolfish eyes that burned with desire.

Gil watched in horror, and as he did so a voice whispered in his mind. It was no more than a thought, but

211

it was not his own. And he felt the presence of the great queen herself, of Carnhaina. *It is time. Shurilgar also seeks to possess her, to return from the dead. One of them will prevail and possess all the power and knowledge of the others. Alithoras will fall in smoke and ruin if that comes to pass.*

Ginsar screamed again. "Master! Help me!" But Gil knew he was not there to help, and that the sorceress was suffering unspeakable torment.

He felt Brand's gaze upon him, sympathy in his expression. The regent understood. And Carnhaina whispered in his mind once more. *There is only one way. It must be done.*

Gil looked at the White Lady. She was so beautiful and yet so sad. She brought joy into the world, and yet he was supposed to destroy her?

She took hold of the end of his sword, raising the tip up toward her. And then she leaned in to speak to him. "You must, Gil. Or everything you love will be destroyed. Alithoras shall fall, and the world after. You must."

"I cannot."

"You must!"

He felt her hands on his where he gripped the hilt of the sword. He felt her magic also, alive and roiling within her. His own responded and leaped up to join with it.

Ginsar screamed. Fire burst from her mouth, and she strode toward him. But he turned his gaze back to the White Lady and looked into her eyes.

"I forgive you," she whispered.

He did not understand, but then he realized that she was stabbed, the length of his sword piercing her body. Dread such as he had never felt settled over him. Had she pushed herself upon the blade? Had he stabbed her?

The White Lady fell to her knees. Ginsar, close by, toppled also to the ground. Her eyes blazed fire and she hissed. Then she spoke, the words she spat formed of many voices all at once. "I hate you!"

Gil was not sure if she directed them at himself or the White Lady. But the White Lady spoke also. "I love you," she whispered. "And this fair land. Protect it. Guard it. Nurture it. And … remember me."

Tears ran down Gil's face. "Always."

"Remember me, but do not mourn. Though I die in this place, yet still I live in that world whence I came." Blood dribbled from the corner of her mouth and she grimaced. "You will be a great king."

"No. I have failed. I have let you down and everyone else."

"You have done what you were born for. Yet there is more yet to come. Remember me … my true name is Halabeth."

She died then, and the light faded from her eyes. But he felt her magic still, felt it rise up and spear through the spinning gateway, dragging the spirits of Ginsar and the Horsemen with her.

There was a flash of white light and a sudden sense of peace. Then it was gone and the world was different from what it had been. The gateway was closed, and grief weighed upon Gil as heavy as a mountain.

Brand leaned on his staff, but he looked out over the battlefield. "It is done," he said. "We have won."

Gil looked around at the devastation of the battlefield. The elug army was routed, pursued by the cavalry. Ginsar's body lay close by, twisted and broken by the powers that had contended to possess it. Of Halabeth, nothing remained save her memory. And that was bitter sweet. He felt a hand on his shoulder and knew by its touch that it was Elrika's. He reached up and put his own hand over it. Then he stood and answered Brand.

"We have won. But at a terrible cost."

Epilogue

Gil sat in Carnhaina's library. The ancient crown of Cardoroth, cut by mystic symbols and decorated with myriad gems, still rested upon his head. Tradition dictated that the new king wore it until midnight on the day of his coronation. He was not going to breach that custom.

Elrika sat with him, and Tainrik also. They both wore the white surcoats of a Durlin. It was a special day for all of them.

He held the diary of the great queen in his hand, unopened.

"Read something," Elrika suggested.

"I'm not sure that I want to. It always seems to fall open at—"

"Yes. At a page that you need to read. Do it, Gil. See what she says to you."

Gil opened the book. It felt heavier in his hand than usual, and it fell open at a point near the beginning. He had read that part before, but he knew he had not ever seen this page. It was neatly written, with lots of white space around the words.

"What does it say?" Tainrik asked.

Gil read aloud, his voice subdued. "Hail, Light of the Realm, for thus is the king of Cardoroth called. Hail, and congratulations. You have triumphed, for now, over the forces of evil. This means you have also won the battle within your soul. And just as there is good and evil in the world, so too that battle plays out inside you. It plays out in all men and women, but especially so in those with

215

magic. Be wary of the dark, but do not fear it. Come to understand it so that you may defeat it when it rises. And it will. I triumphed in the end. My sister did not. Your time of testing is not yet over."

"That's not exactly reassuring," Elrika said.

"You wanted me to read it…"

"Yes. Now keep going. What else does it say?"

Gil did not argue with her. He read on. "And remember, Brand is your friend. He does not believe the two of you shall meet again. He is mistaken. It will not be soon though, for he has many grave trials ahead of him. Spare a thought for him now and then, for while your battles are over for the moment, his are beginning anew." There was a signature, and the name given was Carngin. It was her informal name.

"What else does it say?"

There was a postscript, and he read it out. "Remember, always, that I'm proud of you and love you."

Gil closed the book, and noticed Elrika's gaze upon him.

"Was that so bad?"

"No," he answered. "It wasn't. Though now I worry for Brand."

"Ah," Tainrik said, drawing something from his pocket. "This would be a good time to tell you. He gave me a note for you before he left. I know he's already said his goodbyes, but he gave it to me anyway."

Gil was intrigued. "What does it say?" he asked. "Read it for me, please."

Tainrik cleared his throat. "Gil, we have already said our last farewells, but saying goodbye is hard. Yet this much I need to say, because I did not do so earlier. We may never meet again. I travel now to the land of my birth,

216

the lands of the Duthenor. I know some of what to expect, but I sense there is much more that I do not guess. That does not concern you though. But I want you to understand this. The White Lady was not of this world, nor could she have been happy here, even as I was never truly happy away from my homeland. Yet she lives there, as do her enemies, and the battle between them continues. What you did was … difficult. And you have learned a truth that all of us discover, eventually. Sometimes there are no right choices. Nothing can change that. Nor will it be your last dilemma. So I say this as my final advice to you, and I hope it helps. It is the fate of kings to bear great responsibility. Trust your instincts, but heed the words of wise counselors. Most of all, keep your friends close and keep your enemies guessing … Remember that."

Gil smiled. It was good advice, and he would not forget.

Thus ends *Light of the Realm*. It brings the Son of Sorcery trilogy to a conclusion. Yet Brand must still defeat the usurper. He returns to the land of the Duthenor, but things are not as they seem. Darker forces are at work than he knows, and his life and the future of Alithoras is in greater jeopardy than anyone guesses.

More will be told in:

THE DARK GOD RISES TRILOGY

COMING SOON!

Amazon lists millions of titles, and I'm glad that you discovered this one. But if you'd like to know when I release a new book, instead of leaving it to chance, sign up for my newsletter. I'll send you an email on publication.

Yes please! – Go to www.homeofhighfantasy.com and sign up.

No thanks – I'll take my chances.

Dedication

There's a growing movement in fantasy literature. Its name is noblebright, and it's the opposite of grimdark.

Noblebright celebrates the virtues of heroism. It's an old-fashioned thing, as old as the first story ever told around a smoky campfire beneath ancient stars. It's storytelling that highlights courage and loyalty and hope for the spirit of humanity. It recognizes the dark, the dark in us all, and the dark in the villains of its stories. It recognizes death, and treachery and betrayal. But it dwells on none of these things.

I dedicate this book, such as it is, to that which is noblebright. And I thank the authors before me who held the torch high so that I could see the path: J.R.R. Tolkien, C.S. Lewis, Terry Brooks, David Eddings, Susan Cooper, Roger Taylor and many others. I salute you.

And, for a time, I too will hold the torch as high as I can.

Encyclopedic Glossary

Note: the glossary of each book in this series is individualized for that book alone. Additionally, there is often historical material provided in its entries for people, artifacts and events that are not included in the main text.

Many races dwell in Alithoras. All have their own language, and though sometimes related to one another the changes sparked by migration, isolation and various influences often render these tongues unintelligible to each other.

The ascendancy of Halathrin culture, combined with their widespread efforts to secure and maintain allies against elug incursions, has made their language the primary means of communication between diverse peoples.

For instance, a soldier of Cardoroth addressing a ship's captain from Camarelon would speak Halathrin, or a simplified version of it, even though their native speeches stem from the same ancestral language.

This glossary contains a range of names and terms. Many are of Halathrin origin, and their meaning is provided. The remainder derive from native tongues and are obscure, so meanings are only given intermittently.

Often, Camar names and Halathrin elements are combined. This is especially so for the aristocracy. No

other tribes of men had such long-term friendship with
the immortal Halathrin, and though in this relationship
they lost some of their natural culture, they gained nobility
and knowledge in return.

List of abbreviations:

Azn. Azan

Cam. Camar

Comb. Combined

Cor. Corrupted form

Duth. Duthenor

Hal. Halathrin

Leth. Letharn

Prn. Pronounced

Age of Heroes: A period of Camar history that has
become mythical. Many tales are told of this time. Some
are true while others are not. Yet, even the false ones
usually contain elements of historical fact. Many were the
heroes who walked abroad during this time, and they are
remembered and honored still by the Camar people. The
old days are looked back on with pride, and the
descendants of many heroes walk the streets of Cardoroth
unaware of their heritage and the accomplishments of
their forefathers.

Alith Nien: *Hal.* "Silver river." Has its source in the mountainous lands of Auren Dennath and empties into Lake Alithorin.

Alithoras: *Hal.* "Silver land." The Halathrin name for the continent they settled after their exodus from their homeland. Refers to the extensive river and lake systems they found and their wonder at the beauty of the land.

Anast Dennath: *Hal.* "Stone mountains." Mountain range in northern Alithoras. Source of the river known as the Careth Nien that forms a natural barrier between the lands of the Camar people and the Duthenor and related tribes.

Arach Neben: *Hal.* "West gate." The defensive wall surrounding Cardoroth has four gates. Each is named after a cardinal direction, and each carries a token to represent a celestial object. Arach Neben bears a steel ornament of the Morning Star.

Arell: A famed healer in Cardoroth. Rumored to be Brand's lover.

Aurellin: *Cor. Hal.* The first element means blue. The second is native Camar. Formerly Queen of Cardoroth, wife to Gilhain and grandmother to Gilcarist.

Auren Dennath: *Comb. Duth.* and *Hal. Prn.* Our-ren dennath. "Blue mountains." Mountain range in northern Alithoras. Contiguous with Anast Dennath.

Betrayal: One of the Riders, also called Horsemen, summoned into Alithoras by Ginsar. He represents and instigates betrayal. Yet, in truth, the Riders are spirit-beings from another world. They have been given form and nature within Alithoras by Ginsar. The form provided by her is part of the blood sorcery that binds them to her will. In their own world, they do not bear these names or natures. Yet they are creatures wholly of evil, and though bound by Ginsar they seek to break that bond. Even if defeated, the bond from the summoning persists and the Riders are capable of rising again, even though they are considered dead.

Brand: A Duthenor tribesman. Appointed by the former king of Cardoroth to serve as regent for Gilcarist. By birth, he is the rightful chieftain of the Duthenor people. However, a usurper overthrew his father, killing both him and his wife. Brand, only a youth at the time, swore an oath of vengeance. That oath sleeps, but it is not forgotten, either by Brand or the usurper.

Camar: *Cam. Prn.* Kay-mar. A race of interrelated tribes that migrated in two main stages. The first brought them to the vicinity of Halathar, homeland of the immortal Halathrin; in the second, they separated and established cities along a broad stretch of eastern Alithoras.

Cardoroth: *Cor. Hal. Comb. Cam.* A Camar city, often called Red Cardoroth. Some say this alludes to the red granite commonly used in the construction of its buildings, others that it refers to a prophecy of destruction.

Cardurleth: *Hal.* "Car – red, dur – steadfast, leth – stone." The defensive wall that surrounds Cardoroth. Established soon after the city's founding and constructed of red granite. It looks displeasing to the eye, but the people of the city love it nonetheless. They believe it impregnable and hold that no enemy shall ever breach it – except by treachery.

Careth Nien: *Hal. Prn.* Kareth ni-en. "Great river." Largest river in Alithoras. Has its source in the mountains of Anast Dennath and runs southeast across the land before emptying into the sea. It was over this river (which sometimes freezes along its northern stretches) that the Camar and other tribes migrated into the eastern lands. Much later, Brand came to the city of Cardoroth by one of these ancient migratory routes.

Carnhaina: First element native *Cam*. Second *Hal*. "Heroine." An ancient queen of Cardoroth. Revered as a savior of her people, but to some degree also feared for she possessed powers of magic. Hated to this day by elùgroths because she destroyed their power unexpectedly at a time when their dark influence was rising. According to legend, kept alive mostly within the royal family of Cardoroth, she guards the city even in death and will return in its darkest hour.

Carngin: See Carnhaina.

Conhain: A watchword in use in Cardoroth. Refers to one of the great kings of the Camar peoples who founded a realm in the south of Alithoras.

Death: One of the Riders, also called Horsemen, summoned into Alithoras by Ginsar. He represents and instigates Death. Yet, in truth, the Riders are spirit-beings from another world. They have been given form and nature within Alithoras by Ginsar. The form provided by her is part of the blood sorcery that binds them to her will. In their own world, they do not bear these names or natures. Yet they are creatures wholly of evil, and though bound by Ginsar they seek to break that bond. Even if defeated, the bond from the summoning persists and the Riders are capable of rising again, even though they are considered dead.

Dernbrael: *Hal.* "Sharp-tongued." By some translations, "cunning-tongued." A lord of Cardoroth. Attempted to usurp the throne from Gilcarist. It is said that he is in league with the traitor Hvargil, though this has never been proven.

Drùghoth: *Hal.* First element – black. Second element – that which hastens, races or glides. More commonly called a sending.

Druigbar: *Cam.* A general in Cardoroth's army. In his youth, a runner of extraordinary ability. He possessed speed and endurance, and won the annual race that circuits the Cardurleth seven times out of eight starts.

Durlin: *Hal.* "The steadfast." The original Durlin were the seven sons of the first king of Cardoroth. They guarded him against all enemies, of which there were many, and three died to protect him. Their tradition continued throughout Cardoroth's history, suspended only once, and briefly, some four hundred years ago when it was discovered that three members were secretly in the service of elùgroths. These were imprisoned, but committed suicide while waiting for their trial to commence. It is rumored that the king himself provided them with the knives that they used. It is said that he felt sorry for them and gave them this way out to avoid the shame a trial would bring to their families.

Durlin creed: These are the native Camar words, long remembered and greatly honored, that were uttered by the first Durlin to die while he defended his father, who was also the king, from attack. Tum del conar – El dar tum! Death or infamy – I choose death!

Durlindrath: *Hal.* "Lord of the steadfast." The title given to the leader of the Durlin. For the first time in the history of Cardoroth, that position is held jointly by two people: Lornach and Taingern. Lornach also possesses the title of King's Champion. The latter honor is not held in quite such high esteem, yet it carries somewhat more power. As King's Champion, Lornach is authorized to act in the king's stead in matters of honor and treachery to the Crown.

Duthenor: *Duth. Prn.* Dooth-en-or. "The people." A single tribe, or sometimes a group of closely related tribes melded into a larger people at times of war or disaster, who generally live a rustic and peaceful lifestyle. They are breeders of cattle and herders of sheep. However, when need demands they are bold warriors – men and women alike. Currently ruled by a usurper who murdered Brand's parents. Brand has sworn an oath to overthrow the tyrant and avenge his parents.

Elrika: *Cam.* Daughter of the royal baker. Friend to Gilcarist, and greatly skilled in weapons fighting, especially the long sword. Brand has given instructions to Lornach that she is to be taught all arts of the warrior to the full extent of her ability. He is grooming her to be the first female Durlin in the history of the city.

Elùgrune: *Hal.* Literally "shadowed fortune," but is also translated into "ill fortune" and "born of the dark." In the first two senses it means bad luck. In the third, it connotes a person steeped in shadow and mystery and not to be trusted. In some circles, the term has an additional meaning of "mystic".

Elugs: *Hal.* "That which creeps in shadows." Often called goblins. An evil and superstitious race that dwells in the south of Alithoras, especially the Graèglin Dennath Mountains. They also inhabit portions of the northern mountains of Alithoras, and have traditionally fallen under the sway of elùgroths centered in the region of Cardoroth.

Elùgai: *Hal. Prn.* Eloo-guy. "Shadowed force." The sorcery of an elùgroth.

Elùgroth: *Hal. Prn.* Eloo-groth. "Shadowed horror." A sorcerer. They often take names in the Halathrin tongue in mockery of the lòhren practice to do so.

Esanda: No known etymology for this name. Likewise, Esanda herself is not native to Cardoroth. King Gilhain believed she was from the city of Esgallien, but he was not certain of this. Esanda refuses to answer questions concerning her origins. Regardless of the personal mystery attached to her, she was one of Gilhain's most trusted advisors and soon became so to Brand. She leads a ring of spies utterly devoted to the protection of Cardoroth from the many dark forces that would bring it down.

Esgallien: *Hal. Prn.* Ez-gally-en. "Es – rushing water, gal(en) – green, lien – to cross: place of the crossing onto the green plains." A city founded in antiquity and named after a nearby ford of the Careth Nien. Reports indicate it has fallen to elugs.

Felhain: First element is of unknown *Cam* etymology. Second is *Hal* for "hero". Youngest son of the first king of Cardoroth.

Felargin: *Cam.* A sorcerer, and brother to Ginsar. Acolyte of Shurilgar the elùgroth. Steeped in evil and once lured Brand, Lornach and other adventurers under false pretenses into a quest. Only Brand and Shorty survived the betrayal. Felargin, however, fell victim to the trap he had prepared for the others. Brand was responsible for his death.

Forgotten Queen (the): An epithet of Queen Carnhaina. She was a person of immense power and presence, yet she made few friends in life, and her possession of magic caused her to be mistrusted. For these reasons, memory of her accomplishments faded soon after her passing and only small remnants of her rule are remembered by the populace of Cardoroth.

Garling: *Cam.* A general of Cardoroth's army. Distantly related to the royal family by marriage.

Gil: See Gilcarist.

Gilcarist: *Comb. Cam & Hal.* First element unknown, second "ice." Heir to the throne of Cardoroth and grandson of King Gilhain. According to Carnhaina, his coming was told in the stars. He is also foretold by her as The Savior and The Destroyer. The prophecies mean little to him, for he believes in Brand's view that a man makes his own fate.

Gilhain: *Comb. Cam & Hal.* First element unknown, second "hero." King of Cardoroth before proclaiming Brand regent for Gilcarist, the underage heir to the throne. Husband to Aurellin.

Ginhaina: First element native *Cam.* Second *Hal.* "Heroine." Youngest daughter of the first king of Cardoroth.

Ginsar: *Cam.* A sorceress. Sister to Felargin. Acolyte of Shurilgar the elùgroth. Steeped in evil and greatly skilled in the arts of elùgai, reaching a level of proficiency nearly as great as her master. Rumored to be insane.

Goblins: See elugs.

Graèglin Dennath: *Hal. Prn.* Greg-lin dennath. "Mountains of ash." Chain of mountains in southern Alithoras. Populated by the southern races of elugs.

Halabeth: Etymology unknown. See the White Lady.

Halathar: *Hal.* "Dwelling place of the people of Halath." The forest realm of the immortal Halathrin.

Halathgar: *Hal.* "Bright star." Actually a constellation of two stars. Also called the Lost Huntress.

Halathrin: *Hal.* "People of Halath." A race named after an honored lord who led an exodus of his people to the land of Alithoras in pursuit of justice, having sworn to defeat a great evil. They are human, though of fairer form, greater skill and higher culture than ordinary men. They possess a unity of body, mind and spirit that enables insight and endurance beyond the native races of Alithoras. Said to be immortal, but killed in great numbers during their conflicts in ancient times with the evil they sought to destroy. Those conflicts are collectively known as the Shadowed Wars.

Harath Neben: *Hal.* "North gate." This gate bears a token of two massive emeralds representing the constellation of Halathgar. The gate is also called "Hunter's Gate," for the north road out of the city leads to wild lands of plentiful game. It is said that a stele of Letharn origin was found buried beneath the soil when the foundations of the gate were excavated. No one could read the inscription, but the stele is kept to this day in the gate tower.

Hvargil: Prince of Cardoroth. Younger son of Carangil, former king of Cardoroth. Exiled by Carangil for treason after it was discovered he plotted with elùgroths to assassinate his older half-brother, Gilhain, and prevent him from ascending the throne. He gathered a band about him in exile of outlaws and discontents. Most came from Cardoroth but others were drawn from the southern Camar cities. He fought with the invading army of elugs against Cardoroth in the previous war.

Immortals: See Halathrin.

Letharn: *Hal.* "Stone raisers. Builders." A race of people that in antiquity conquered most of Alithoras. Now, only faint traces of their civilization endure.

Lethrin: *Hal.* "Stone people." Creatures of legend sometimes called trolls. Renowned for their size and strength. Tunnelers and miners.

Lòhren: *Hal. Prn.* Ler-ren. "Knowledge giver – a counselor." Other terms used by various nations include wizard, druid and sage.

Lòhrengai: *Hal. Prn.* Ler-ren-guy. "Lòhren force." Enchantment, spell or use of mystic power. A manipulation and transformation of the natural energy inherent in all things. Each use takes something from the user. Likewise, some part of the transformed energy infuses them. Lòhrens use it sparingly, elùgroths indiscriminately.

Lornach: *Cam.* A former Durlin and now joint Durlindrath. Also holds the title of King's Champion. Friend to Brand, and often called by his nickname of "Shorty."

Lothgern: A general of Cardoroth's army. Also a breeder of some of the finest horses in the realm. These he sells, at exorbitant prices, to cavalry soldiers. The soldiers complain bitterly about the price, but most do not stint on the fee. The reputation of the horses is paramount. The black stallion owned by Brand was foaled in Lothgern's stables.

Magic: Mystic power. See lòhrengai and elùgai.

Nightborn: See elùgrune.

Olekgar: *Comb. Cam & Hal.* First element unknown, second "star." A disciple of Ginsar. Born outside Cardoroth yet descended from the city's aristocracy.

Otherworld: Camar term for a mingling of half-remembered history, myth and the spirit world.

Sometimes used interchangeably with the term "Age of Heroes."

Raithlin: *Hal.* "Range and report people." A scouting and saboteur organization. Derived from ancient contact with, and the teachings of, the Halathrin. Their skills are legendary throughout Alithoras.

Sandy: See Esanda.

Sellic Neben: *Hal.* "East gate." This gate bears a representation, crafted of silver and pearl, of the moon rising over the sea.

Shorty: See Lornach.

Shurilgar: *Hal.* "Midnight star." An elùgroth. One of the most puissant sorcerers of antiquity. Known to legend as the Betrayer of Nations.

Sorcerer: See Elùgroth.

Sorcery: See elùgai.

Stillness in the Storm: A mental state sought by many warriors. It is that sense of the mind being separate from the body. If achieved, it frees the warrior from emotions such as fear and pain that hinder physical performance. The body, in its turn, moves and reacts by trained instinct alone allowing the skill of the warrior to flow unhindered to the surface. Those who have perfected the correct mental state feel as though they can slow down the passage of time during a fight. It is an illusion, yet the state of feeling that way is a combat advantage.

Surcoat: An outer garment usually worn over chainmail. The Durlin surcoat is unadorned white, which is a tradition carried down from the order's inception.

Taingern: *Cam*. A former Durlin. Friend to Brand, and now joint Durlindrath. Once, in company of Brand, saved the tomb of Carnhaina from defilement and robbery by an elùgroth.

Time: One of the Riders, also called Horsemen, summoned into Alithoras by Ginsar. He represents Time – specifically as manifested by the aging process. Yet, in truth, the Riders are spirit-beings from another world. They have been given form and nature within Alithoras by Ginsar. The form provided by her is part of the blood sorcery that binds them to her will. In their own world, they do not bear these names or natures. Yet they are creatures wholly of evil, and though bound by Ginsar they seek to break that bond. Even if defeated, the bond from the summoning persists and the Riders are capable of rising again, even though they are considered dead.

Tower of Halathgar: In life, a place of study of Queen Carnhaina. In death, her resting place. Unusually, her sarcophagus rests on the tower's parapet beneath the stars.

Unlach Neben: *Hal.* "South gate." This gate bears a representation of the sun, crafted of gold, beating down upon an arid land. Said to signify the southern homeland of the elugs, whence the gold of the sun was obtained by an adventurer of old.

Ùhrengai: *Hal. Prn.* Er-ren-guy. "Original force." The primordial force that existed before substance or time.

233

War: One of the Riders, also called Horsemen, summoned into Alithoras by Ginsar. He represents conflict and battle. Yet, in truth, the Riders are spirit-beings from another world. They have been given form and nature within Alithoras by Ginsar. The form provided by her is part of the blood sorcery that binds them to her will. In their own world, they do not bear these names or natures. Yet they are creatures wholly of evil, and though bound by Ginsar they seek to break that bond. Even if defeated, the bond from the summoning persists and the Riders are capable of rising again, even though they are considered dead.

White Lady: A being of spirit drawn into Alithoras as an unintended consequence of Ginsar's summoning of the Riders.

Wizard: See lòhren.

Wych-wood: A general description for a range of supple and springy timbers. Some hardy varieties are prevalent on the poisonous slopes of the Graèglin Dennath Mountains, and are favored by elùgroths as instruments of sorcery.

About the author

I'm a man born in the wrong era. My heart yearns for faraway places and even further afield times. Tolkien had me at the beginning of *The Hobbit* when he said, ". . . one morning long ago in the quiet of the world . . ."

Sometimes I imagine myself in a Viking mead-hall. The long winter night presses in, but the shimmering embers of a log in the hearth hold back both cold and dark. The chieftain calls for a story, and I take a sip from my drinking horn and stand up . . .

Or maybe the desert stars shine bright and clear, obscured occasionally by wisps of smoke from burning camel dung. A dry gust of wind marches sand grains across our lonely campsite, and the wayfarers about me stir restlessly. I sip cool water and begin to speak.

I'm a storyteller. A man to paint a picture by the slow music of words. I like to bring faraway places and times to life, to make hearts yearn for something they can never have, unless for a passing moment.

36809170R00137

Printed in Great Britain
by Amazon